Cover Design by Susan Segovia-Munoz

First Edition 2024

ISBN: 979-8-9917784-3-5

Library of Congress Control Number: 2024923288

This book is dedicated to those who said we would fail. Thank you for your giving us the chance to prove you wrong...

Guy Castle is a man who's had enough. Once a highly skilled commando and covert intelligence operative, he's left that life behind—worn out, burned out, and haunted by ghosts that won't stay buried. After years of dangerous missions and countless brushes with death, Guy wants nothing more than to live in solitude, far away from the violence and betrayal that have defined his past.

But the past doesn't stay quiet for long. When a cryptic message arrives, dragging him back into a shadowy world he thought he'd escaped, Guy is forced to dust off his old skills and play a deadly game against forces that want him eliminated. Thrust into a high-stakes conspiracy where no one can be trusted and every move could be his last, Guy must navigate a maze of ruthless enemies and dangerous secrets—while grappling with his own inner demons.

The deeper he's pulled into this dark web, the more his old instincts resurface, pushing him to confront the trauma and regrets he's tried to bury. As new enemies close in and long-buried secrets come to light, Guy must fight not only for survival but for redemption. But with the line between friend and foe blurred, he'll have to decide how far he's willing to go—and what he's willing to sacrifice—to make it out alive.

This is a story of grit, vengeance, and the relentless fight for freedom, filled with heart-stopping twists, visceral action, dark humor and moments of unexpected humanity. For Guy

Castle, every victory comes at a price, and in the end, it may cost him everything.

Strap in for a pulse-pounding thrill ride where the stakes are life and death, and every page ignites the fire in your soul. Experience the adrenaline, the danger, and the highs and lows that only come when your...

Soul is on Fire.

Contents

Chapter One

Roaring like an inferno, my soul is on fire.

Gasping, I catch my breath; the sound echoing in the silence. My hand jerks upward as I wipe my sweaty brow, attempting to calm myself. I feel my heart rapidly pounding against my chest as my chiseled body shudders with unease. The feverish burning sensation gets more intense with each passing second. Confused, I snapped into a sitting position. I'm wet from head to toe, even my sheets. The three dog tags secured to me by a chain wrapped in paracord are stuck against my muscular chest. I peel them away and then tightly hold them between my fingers, my knuckles turning white. A tear rolls down my face when I hear the familiar clink that reminds me of the only thing I have left.

My scars.

It's 4:18 am, and I know I won't be going back to sleep. So, I get up and stretch for a moment, working out the morning kinks. I strut over to the full-length mirror and can't help but admire my morning wood. Let me tell you, the many years of military and secret government service have sculpted me into a lean, mean, muscular middle-aged man. While other guys my age would probably give up about now, I'll never change my routine, since I still enjoy turning heads while jogging alongside the bikini-clad hotties on the boardwalk.

It pays to have great abs.

Alley, my best friend, a loyal German Shepherd, is looking at me from her oversized bed. I don't know why, but some people find it amusing to have a dog as a best friend, but they have no clue how smart German Shepherds are. Plus, we have history. If Alley could reach the pedals, I know she'd get my drunk ass home safely and without involving the cops each and every time.

She gets up, stretches, shakes, and gives me the *"feed me now eyes."* She really cracks me up, and believe it or not, my best friend has saved my life.

More than once.

You see, I was having a beer down at Charlie's a while back, and I'm talking about the local Bar and Grill, not the weirdo down the street with all those comic books. I'm sitting, talking to the bartender, and having a brew, and I get a craving for one of their famous burgers.

My mouth waters just thinking about it. So, I placed my order and when it was ready, the chef stepped away from the grill and out of the kitchen. He slid the plate down the counter, and my meal lands right in front of me, like a bar scene in an old black and white movie. I pick up my grub, head outside to the patio - plate in one hand and a pitcher of beer in the other, then grab a seat at an empty table.

I take a huge bite out of my burger, and for some odd reason, I start thinking about the new server. She's standing a few feet away from me and lurking around the corner. As she takes a couple steps in my direction, I glance at her name tag: Jenny.

Well, I guess the best way to describe Jenny would be as a somewhat attractive woman. But what's strange is that she wears a ton of makeup, and it looks like she's wearing a mask. Don't get me wrong, she can be a sweetheart, but she'll never be mine. Plus, the only time she served me, she was sweating so much that it brought on a flashback of my undercover time in South America. Then, when she brought me my beer, she tripped and spilled the entire thing all over me.

I shake off the misery of that thought, and my mind begins to wander. I'm brought back to reality when I see a stray, matted mess of a mongrel or something, just sitting there staring at me, you know, all sad and everything.

Now I can be a mean motherfucker, but I'm no monster, so I toss him my burger, and he flinches. It broke my heart when I saw him shying away from the food. It was no secret that this mangy dog had never known love.

What a fucked-up world we live in.

But you know what? That dog sucked it up in one sloppy gulp as soon as hunger took over. It surprised us both. The scrounge looked at me and gave me the *"what's up"* chin lift, and then disappeared around the corner.

Good luck, buddy.

When I turned back, I caught Jenny staring at me from across the patio. I saw her fumble with her order pad, almost dropping it. I cracked a quick smile and then glanced away. Nope, not for me. She's not my type, but I guess she'd do in a pinch on a rough night. A port in every storm, they say. And anyway, after downing a couple of pitchers she's not that bad looking.

Glancing back toward her, I motioned for another round, and when she returned with my beer, she set it on the table and walked away. But then she turned around, and for a second, she locked eyes with me. It was so awkward. And you know what? I could swear I've seen her before. Jenny looks oddly familiar, but I can't place where or if we've ever met. Anyway, there was something suspicious about the way she was acting.

I poured myself another beer because seeing that dog was just plain depressing, and after downing that one, another mug and then another. Before I knew it, that turned into sixteenth, oh-four nonsense and complete gibberish.

Shit! Wasted again.

My plan was to catch a brew and maybe a burger, but unfortunately, I missed the turnoff and sped in the opposite direction of the path of *"the right thing to do"*.

It's a problem, I agree.

But it sure as shit beats being fucking mundane! Please, shoot me in the head right away, if you ever catch me wearing Crocs and driving a beige minivan.

I mumbled something to that effect as I stumbled down the sidewalk and into the back alley to water the graffiti.

A wise man once said, you don't really buy beer; you more or less rent it.

I'm usually savvy about my surroundings, hypervigilant and all, but this was Charlie's, and I was swaying around, pissing on my boots, sloshed.

So, when two shit birds came up from behind, they caught me off guard.

"Got a light?"

As I turned to respond, someone struck the back of my head with something. Now, I was surprised, but I'm no milquetoast, so I looked at them with murder in my eyes.

The only issue was that there were two of each of them, and whether two or four, they got me good. Damn, I've got to stop wearing these alcohol goggles, because they just don't do the trick. No problem, I'll just go rogue on them all.

Good old drunk logic.

I swing at the first guy, a punk with terrible skin. So, just to keep things simple, we'll call him Pimples. He's got a short rat-fink friend I find hard not to call Nibbles. When my fist connects with Pimple's jaw, the blow glances off, throwing me off balance and causing me to fall. As I lay there sprawled out on the ground, Nibbles charges in and tries to kick me in the head. And although you might find it difficult to believe, I was accurate and caught his foot.

Big mistake, motherfucker!

Man, I torqued that foot like I was spinning a top. I heard a wet crack, followed by a high-pitched scream as Nibbles flopped on top of me. We're tangled up in a crazy wrestler's knot when Pimples sprouts a pair of pock-marked balls and jumps in to help his cheese-eating friend. Nibbles is wailing like a chick on crack, holding his mangled ankle together, as I elbow it one more time for good luck. I think this puts him out, but I couldn't be sure because I was losing consciousness myself.

What the hell?

As my perspective flips 90 degrees and my head hits the ground, I see Pimples rushing toward me again, and everything fades to black.

Chapter Two

A few things registered as I came to: water dripping from somewhere and a dog panting. It was soothing, but it kind of threw me for a loop.

Wait, a dog panting?

I gradually open my bloodshot eyes, and it takes a minute for my lagging brain to catch up.

What happened? Oh, yeah.

I lifted myself slowly and saw the mangy mutt from before lounging by my legs with his head on my lap. My first thought was that he wanted another burger. Pimples and Nibbles were gone, and there's no one else in the alley besides this dirty dog and me. Looking up, I see the bright neon lights of this smoggy city flashing in the distance.

Damn, this would make one hell of a country song.

My canine companion makes a worried little sound, but his eyes say it all. He's genuinely concerned about me.

Is that a good thing or a bad thing?

I stabilized myself on the asphalt and returned to an upright position next to my newfound friend. How did I get out of the scrape I was in? I was sure Pimples had me. That's when I saw the bloody ripped-up leather jacket that he had been wearing. I look at the stray, and he looks back at the jacket, then at me, then back at the torn and shredded leather, and then he yawns. I'm not sure what that means in dog language, but I'll take it as if it was all in a good day's work.

"Good dog, thanks."

I'd love to pat him on the head to thank him, but he's so filthy. My hands have dry blood all over them, and my knuckles are cracked open. Although, I do make a mental note to buy him another burger if we ever meet again. When I walk out of the alley, I get a strange feeling, like I'm being shadowed, so I turned back to check. I see it's the dog and now I feel like he's my escort and walking me home. A black car with dark-tinted windows passes by and flashes the lights twice before disappearing around the corner. I shake it off as if it's just another drunk driver finding his way home. It's not long before we arrive at my small walk-down.

Now, I'm stuck in a moral dilemma. What should I do?

The mutt looks at me and tilts his head. My resistance shatters, and I know it's going to get messy, but I cave anyway.

"Oh, alright, come on in."

And he just sits there. He doesn't move at all. What the hell? I take a step toward him, and he takes a step back.

Oh, he's leery.

"It's okay, bud...I got you."

I head toward the stairwell, walk down the steps, unlock my door, and enter. I return a minute later with a nice, thick steak. I've been meaning to grill it for quite some time now but fuck it. The boy's getting it raw, blood and all. When that dog saw me heading back up with that fat slab of moo, his eyes popped wide open. I'm telling you; he looked like a sick junkie finding a bag of dope - *the Devil's Dandruff.*

I pulled out my pocketknife, flicked it open, and he jumped back at the sound.

Wow, you have had a rough life.

I cut off a hefty sized chunk with a razor-sharp, tanto-style blade and gently lobbed it in his direction. He intercepted the meaty ball mid-throw and swallowed it whole.

Nice catch!

We bond like this for a minute or two, me throwing the steak in different directions and him catching every single piece before it hits the ground.

This dog should play for the Yankees.

Devouring the last bite of rib eye, he sits before me, wagging his tail, and then lets out a little burp.

It's becoming that time of night that turns into the morning as we hang out together, a chill seeping into us both. I've had the front door open for so long that I'm sure there's no heat left in my small walk-down basement apartment. The place is nothing fancy, but the sidewalk-level window lets me see people coming.

The skills I've gained over the years came with many sacrifices but pay was never one of them. Uncle Sam loved his little nephew and always made it rain. If the analogy is a nest egg, I have a zoo. Yet, I choose to live simply and move lightly; it works for me as long as my bass guitar travels right along with me. All is well.

Punk Rocker from the get-go.

We have been spending time together on the steps for so long my ass is cold and it's fallen asleep. I stand up, and he follows suit. We both headed into my apartment with a tired yawn and a stretch. He sniffs the air, looking around as I follow him. He stops in front of the amp and my bass guitar.

Please don't piss on my teenage memories.

He smells the carpet and the walls, then stops an extra-long time at the couch, sniffing some butt, I suppose. He looks at me, and I look at him. I know exactly what he's thinking.

Not the couch boy. You're filthy!

Well, he jumps up and lies down, making himself right at home. His ears are back, his tail wagging quickly, and he's kind of looking at me like he's waiting for something terrible to happen. I sauntered over to him with my hands open. He licks his chops and yawns nervously. I softly placed a hand beside him, and he extended his snout to sniff it. After he felt satisfied, I gently placed my hand on his head.

He softly growled, as if to say, "Do not betray my trust."

With my hands sitting against his head, I rub my thumb against his matted fur.

"You're a good boy."

Chapter Three

I placed my knife in the sink to wash it later and headed to the bedroom, keeping the door open. As I enter, I pull my filthy gutter-soaked T-shirt off my muscular body and throw it in the trash. I shower quickly and examine my head, feeling a lump on the back of it.

Motherfuckers!

I swear, I never look for it, but trouble always finds me. Like I'm some kind of magnet to danger, connecting me to every shady situation. I threw on some shorts and headed to bed, done with this messed up day. Shit! Now I'm horny and alone, but I can't find the motivation to do anything about it, so I just crash out. As I tossed and turned, I thought about that new barmaid at Charlie's, Jenny. I think she's in her late thirties, but I can't really tell. She's the type of woman who looks much older than her actual age, likely due to all that crap she wears on her face. I love all types and sizes of women, but I don't think she could handle what I bring to the table, bed, stairs, or wherever. I'd hate to ruin the poor thing. She seems so sad and displaced, which makes her a bit hard on the eyes. Like I said, there's something odd about Jenny. With a sigh, I fall into a restless sleep.

Will this ever end?

Finding myself in a TV studio that appears to have come from the 1950s, I look around. Suddenly, I'm on the stage of a game show, and standing behind a podium as one of the guests. There's no color whatsoever. Everything is black and white.

Fade in:

The audience CLAPS.

A tall circus barker-type fellow in a tight striped suit smiles overly at the camera; his teeth grow sharp and pointy as each second passes. The man's powdered features are stretched tight, and his pupils are glowing. His hair is parted painfully straight in the middle, and it shines so much it looks like a plastic cap.

"Good evening, ladies, and gentlemen, welcome back to the show where we ask..."

At this, he dramatically leans in the audience's direction, hand to his ear as they shout back at him.

"How much of your life is yours?"

"Folks that's right! It's the show that wants to know! You know?"

The audience LAUGHS.

"Our contestant today is none other than this guy right here! Say hi, Guy!"

"Uh."

PAUSE.

Waiting for an answer, the host squints, and his lip curls upward.

The audience LAUGHS again.

"Now, Guy..."

He walks over to me, almost tripping, and rests his skinny arm on the podium. He crosses his ankles and honks a weird clown horn about three times before gliding to the other side. While his back was to the audience, I watched his face suddenly contort into a mask of hatred and pure rage. He looks at me with venom and disgust. When he turns around, he's again wearing that way too big of a smile. He talks to the audience, but his eyes are on me.

"...you think your life is all your own! Do you? Well, let's find out! Shall we?"

Weird music plays, and it sounds like a trumpet is blowing the fuck out of a kick drum. The host shuffles an odd tap dance as the light starts strobing and moving around like a rave party. He waves his hands spastically over his head and starts singing.

"Skiddle dee-dee, snap doodle me, tell us how much of your life we will see?"

My body hurtles across the stage toward the host and slams into him, bulldozing him into the back wall. He hits so hard that he suspended in the air for a second or two before pirouetting plummeting to the floor. This causes the wood backing to splinter and the set pieces to scatter everywhere.

The audience APPLAUSES.

The host stands up, bleeding from a cut above his creepy eye. He sings again, then twirls his limp body around me like a broken marionette.

"Gonna hit me, gonna break me, violence is all he decries. Try to be cool, try to be nice, because everyone you love hates you and dies."

He turns away, then suddenly looks at me and screams.

"All you know is the icy feeling of the fire!"

Shut up! Shut up! Shut up!

I fell off the podium and onto the floor, feeling like I was being pulled backwards and 1000 mph, before realizing I hadn't moved an inch. I was cold, and everything around me was so quiet and still.

How long have I been like this?

I noticed fog emitting from the floor. I glanced back up, and the game show host was gone. The podium was now on the tile and covered in a thin frost.

No! Not after that.

But then, I saw snow falling in the studio. First, softly, then harder and harder until the wind howls, and a blizzard pounds down upon me. I notice flames in the distance and feel sandwiched between the two opposing elements—heat on one side and ice on the other. A sensation that feels like I'm being buried in a metal grave of liquid methane, helium, and liquid nitrogen.

There is fire and death everywhere.

I wake up with a jolt, not even realizing I've jumped out of bed. I stand there holding my aching head, shaking, confused for a moment. I feel a sharp chill against my wet skin, as if it's trying to drain the life from my fragile soul. I grab a t-shirt from the floor and wipe away the sweat. Goosebumps race over my toned biceps, making their way up to my shoulders and then to my neck, as if to strangle me. I grab ahold of the metal dog tags, feeling the warmth from my feverish skin, and I know I'll never be able to get rid of these ghosts.

I walk into my little living room and head to my smaller kitchen. I grab my water bottle and take a long gulp. Sometimes, when I'm elevated, drinking the water and being present in that moment is enough to pull me through and center me once again. I hear a whine from behind me and turned around to see the mangy dog just sitting there, panting. I see his crusty eyes look at the water bottle in my hand and then at me, staring with a, *"Where's my water?"* type of expression.

It's the eyebrows. They get me every time.

I feel bad I didn't think about him needing water last night, but I filled a bowl and set it down on the old linoleum floor of my kitchen. He prances over to it and laps at the water. This goes on for about a minute before he stops, gags for a second, and then drinks a little more.

Sheesh, he was thirsty.

"We'll need to get you some gear if you're moving in, bud..."

His head tilts to the side as if he's processing that.

"...and a bath."

He looks the other way at this, and I chuckle.

"Oh, you'll learn that word, but first, you need a name. Hmm. How about Bob?"

He barks as if he agrees. Okay, that's settled. Now let's get some breakfast.

"You hungry, Bob?"

He's watching my every move, and I can tell he's still trying to figure me out. I changed into some sweats, a somewhat clean T-shirt, socks, and running shoes. Then, grabbing my things, I look over at my new roommate.

"Wanna go on a run?"

I headed to the door, opened it, and looked back at him. He looked worried, and I could tell he thought I was going to kick him out. He lays down and lets out a slight whimper. His tail is wagging rapidly from anxiety.

"All right, Bob. Just stay here. I'll get some stuff and be right back. Cool?"

He looks at me before yawning, and I wonder why I'm conversing with a dog.

Have I gone crazy? And if I had, would I even know?

I headed out the door with these thoughts running through my mind.

Chapter Four

I've always hated mornings, but I do look forward to the run once I get out there and start stretching. I can see why some people don't like to jog. But ever since I've found my rhythm, I've enjoyed the solitary contemplation that comes with the steady slab of my shoes against the pavement.

I hooked a left, and before I knew it, I was on the board-walk in front of Charlie's, hungry and ready for breakfast. I see Charlie greeting a few customers at the hostess stand, always a smile on his face. He's a successful businessman, staying open 24 hours a day, serving drinks and food round the clock.

I head inside, enjoying the smell of fresh coffee and pan-cakes, and grab a table by the wall.

Always the last booth, it's a known fact.

I'm chuckling under my breath as Jenny, of all people, comes up to the table. Because of that, she looks at me funny, and I shift the direction of what's happening inside my head.

"Hey Jenny, I was just thinking about how much I love this place. It cracks me up."

"You know what cracks me up?"

"Huh?"

"Customers stiffing Charlie."

Flashing an insincere grin, she shoves her hand in her pocket and grabs my bill. I notice a flash of sparkle and see that she has a fancy gold and diamond dog collar buckled around her wrist.

Yikes...her face went beat red.

She looks away, fanning herself with the check, then turns back.

"Especially the ones who down six pitchers of beer within a couple hours. I would expect more from someone like you."

I hide my head in shame, realizing that she was talking about last night.

Oops.

I never came back in to settle up. I just wandered home with my new pal and forgot all about my tab.

"Sorry, I had a little drunken emergency. Here, I'll take that."

She slams my bill down on the table right in front of me. Then, realizing she might lose restraint, she takes a deep breath and smooths the sleeves of her shirt.

"Don't mess with me today. I'm working overtime, a double shift."

I pay and then pray that I never have to deal with this woman again.

As I'm waiting in my usual seat, a cute little server named Lorraine takes my order. At first glance, it looks like she's a living doll, you know, a little sweetheart. But once you get to know her, you find out she's a mouthy little bitch. When she came back to my table with my breakfast, a number three special, she couldn't help but spill all the latest gossip.

"Oh, my goodness! You'll never believe this!"

Not listening...

"This morning...earlier...a strange looking woman stormed up to Jenny and pulled her into the corner. Jenny looked so frightened. Oh, I know this sounds crazy, but I think I heard the woman say something about a bunny rabbit or a dog and, also something about Aunt Harriet! Can you believe that?"

Still not listening...

"I think she said that her aunt died! But I'm not 100% sure because I really couldn't hear much more."

Well, that's a good thing.

I caught a bit of luck when someone from a couple of tables down called for Lorraine. Now, I could finally eat in peace, at least that's what I thought. Then my brain tricks me into thinking that a heavy dose of perfume is heading my way and at a rapid pace.

It's not a trick.

I see Jenny coming my way, and when she passes Lorraine, she gives her the stink eye, and then stops at my table for a second.

Why is she so sweaty?

"Don't forget to pay Lorraine."

I can't control my tongue, especially after seeing that fancy collar around her wrist.

"Hubba bubba jig jigs. **You** have a dog?"

Jenny rubs her sleeves, turns toward Lorraine, then back to me. She seems very dissatisfied with her coworker.

"Not that it's any of your business, but yes, I do; I now have a dog. My Bunny is at The Paw Spa as we speak, getting the Luxury Lavender Package."

The Paw Spa. Hmm.

Jenny storms away, leaving her scent lingering in the air. That woman is annoying, but let me tell you, her absence has put me in a pretty good mood. But I have to wait a couple of seconds for the air to clear before I finish eating my protein and carbs.

And yes, I paid my bill.

Chapter Five

I walk back to my little whack-shack and call The Paw Spa, not knowing exactly what to expect. The phone rings about three times, and then a woman answers.

"Greetings! Thank you for calling The Paw Spa! How may I be of assistance?"

The woman spoke in such a peculiar way that I felt like I was calling to make reservations for a vacation at a fancy resort.

"Uh, I'd like to bring my boy Bob in for a bath and a haircut."

There was a brief pause, and for a second, I thought she hung up on me. Or maybe we had disconnected.

"Excuse me, a bath and a haircut? This is a posh, prestigious, high-end grooming spa, sir. Here at The Paw Spa, our main priority is to primp, pamper, prime, perfume and polish, your pup to perfection."

What the fuck have I gotten myself into this time?

The woman droned on, telling me everything about the extravagant and pricey canine establishment. When she paused for a second, I grabbed the opportunity and got an appointment for Bob. Fortunately, someone had canceled, and I snatched up the open slot. We were scheduled to be there in about half an hour.

"Come on, Bob. Let's go get groomed!"

Bob wouldn't budge, so I headed over to the refrigerator and grabbed a package of bologna, you know, as an incentive. I had to bribe him to get off the couch, out the door, and into my beloved Jeep. It's a good thing I bought the extra-large package of b-o-l-o-n-g-a.

I suspect he's on to this game and controlling it.

We arrived at the spot, and with another slice of mystery meat, I was able to get Bob out and onto the sidewalk without a scratch. I swear, I love my Jeep so much that if anything were to happen to it, it would kill me. I'd be so much more than just devastated.

She's my one and only, and always will be.

An unhealthy dose of foo-foo bombarded us when we entered the plush pet parlor. My eyes watered, and I had to blink away the tears, unsure when the mothership had picked me up.

An older woman approached us hesitantly with a stern demeanor and an air of class disdain - a hatchet-faced biddy wearing three-thousand-dollar shoes, working at a dog grooming palace.

Seriously?

She eyed me up and down with a judgmental look on her face.

"Sir, are you lost? You must be in the wrong location."

She says the last part like she's a fucking Shakespearean actress, and I do have to agree I'm in the wrong place. A few people turn to watch the new drama unfold.

"This here's Bob. We're here a little early, and I'd like you to hook him up!"

I'm still blinking away at the chemical weapons deployed in the name of canine vanity.

"Oh my! Sir, I do fear it would be quite a challenge. An impossible feat, I must say, even for the prestigious professionals here at The Paw Spa."

The woman looked as though she were in shock, like I had just asked her to power wash and landscape the entire city.

"Don't worry. He's a good boy."

The prospect horrified her, and not only did she see the shape Bob was in, but she could smell him from across the room. I'm sure she didn't like my new friend stinking up this poofy joint.

I looked down at Bob and grin, watching as he sniffs the carpet, oblivious to our current class struggle.

Let's try a different angle.

"I have an appointment at 1:30."

I say that with such finesse, I could feel my teeth itch.

"The appointment for Bob has been canceled, sir. We cannot provide service for your dog. He is much too dirty and oh so matted. I do not know how, or even if you can, but I cannot tell one end from the other!"

She says the last part assertively, and I lost my patience.

"Well lady, then do both ends! Who are you anyway, the manager?"

She looked like she had just snorted a lemon.

"I am the centers foremost expert on canine luxuries and lotions, and I, of course, hold all the important and most significant certifications."

Impressive. Lady, I don't give a fuck.

"May I please see the manager...ma'am?"

I'm trying my best not to lose my cool.

Because I wanted to be the better smelling person.

Spinning on her toe like a pissed-off ice skater, she glides away.

I looked around as I waited for the manager. The entire space looked like Victoria's Secret had thrown up in a fancy ice cream parlor - an elaborate display of extravagance.

Why am I here?

Then I looked down at my dog and saw him panting happily. This must be the first time in a long time, if ever, that he felt accepted and wasn't being shooed away or yelled at.

"Don't listen to her, Bob. You'll have your appointment. I'm getting you the best package available."

I browse the menu on the wall behind the front desk and decide to get Bob, the Supreme-Ultra-Extreme-Extensive-Expensive-Spa-Experience for large to extra-large dogs.

I glanced over at the glass shelves by the door containing bottles that looked like they all held magic genies. This place is something else. The floor is carpeted, which I found to be an interesting choice seeing dogs piss and poop wherever they want. They don't care about pile count. A few women are standing around like models, very statuesque, and they're wearing funny-looking clothes I'm sure are very expensive.

Poor ladies! You look like Jackson Pollock just spewed paint over each of your skinny frames. Eat something, please. Looking at you makes me hungry.

I turned back to the counters and cases and saw a pair of 14 karat gold grooming shears.

Stainless steel isn't good enough?

And then I shit you not. A small man who looked like he had just stepped out of a comic strip wobbled up to me. And just like in a cartoon, bongo music played in my head with each awkward step he took.

He's squeaked out something that sounded like a party horn or a kazoo.

"How may I help you, sir?"

Don't laugh...no, do not laugh.

"I'm here to get the Crown Prince's dog washed. They just returned from a trip abroad."

When the manager looked at Bob, he caught him off guard, and Bob also felt surprised.

"That won't be a problem, will it? It certainly would be a shame if the Prince dropped his account here."

I say this last part while looking across the room at my nemesis, Hatchet.

I hope they don't check.

The manager looks at Bob again.

"And exactly which Prince are we talking about?"

I laugh. I just couldn't keep it in any longer.

"Sir, you're funny! I didn't say a Prince; I said the Prince and I'm losing my patience."

I leaned in toward the little man, intimidating him, sending him right back into the comic strip he had initially hopped out from.

"Oh yes, right away, sir."

He chirps for Mrs. James to come up to the front.

"Mrs. James, please see our client to Suite One."

Hatchet, at this point, has turned about 50 shades of gray, just kidding...white by this time, and she can only obey the manager.

"Right away, sir."

She walks away and returns a moment later with a leash. As she approaches Bob, he growls. She stops, looks at me, and I shrug.

"I don't think he wants that."

She's irritated and shoots me a disdainful glance, and I feel sorry for old Hatchet. She can't help that her kingdom was built on lies.

"Come on Bob, this way."

Bob's right behind me as I walk down the hall. Hatchet skates past and leads us to Suite One like a begrudging librarian taking a heathen to her favorite book. On our way to the room, I overheard someone talking to a dog in one of the other suites.

"Oh, Bunny bun bun! Bunny Fowler! You lucky little heiress! It's so hard calling you Bunny Carpenter! It just doesn't sound right."

I peeked into the suite for a hot second and saw a ridiculously small white mini poodle flossing a new silver collar with diamonds.

Wait, haven't I seen a collar like that before?

We arrived at Suite One with no more drama and entered an area that was a mix between the operating room from that one hospital TV show and the International Space Station. Tools surround a central raised dais where the dog gets groomed. The room contains various styling essentials such as clippers, shavers, hoses, valves, and a control panel.

As I lead my matted friend to the platform, he looks at me, his eyes filled with questions. I don't want another lengthy conversation with him, so I throw more bologna up onto the spot. Bob takes the bait and jumps up without hesitation. I hear Hatchet gasp, and I think I just sinned in her temple of fragrance and control.

She looks at her current dilemma with disgust, pulling out a face mask and then putting it on. She walks around the grooming table, examining Bob from every angle. He makes a little noise that I interpret as nerves.

"It's okay, boy."

Hatchet bursts into laughter as she looks up from her studies.

"Dear Sir, your ignorance bewilders me. Oh my, Bob is not a boy. He is a girl!"

She smiles and tilts her head a little to the side.

"You would think the Crown Prince would know that."

I feel a cold shock hit my body as I sweat what she'll say next. But to my surprise, she smiles and winks at me, then gets straight to work.

She respected the hustle.

Game always recognizes game, and I now see Mrs. James in a new light.

Chapter Six

After prepaying and including a generous tip, I'm now waiting at the end of the hallway, leaning against the wall like a cool guy. I'm scrolling through the news articles on my phone when one catches my eye. It's about the death of a woman named Harriet Fowler. What sticks out is that it was so close to this area and that she was a wealthy businesswoman with a very shady past.

Out of the corner of my eye, I noticed a few women gawking at me.

Not a chance in hell, ladies. You'd eat me alive.

Then, turning toward the other side of the lobby, I see Mrs. James walking down the hallway with the most beautiful German shepherd I've ever seen in my life.

Now, that's a gorgeous dog.

She stops in front of me.

"How's it going, Mrs. James? Any chance you can give me an ETA?"

I hate waiting. Time just draaaaaaaags.

I think I might have some type of hyperactive whatchamacallit, but I've never allowed anyone to pin me down long enough to check for any malfunction.

She looks at me, cracks a smile, and shakes her head.

"My dear boy, you are so silly! I certainly feel sorry for you. You do know your girl Bob needs her shots, and of course, to be spayed, right?"

Mrs. James looks down at the dog, shaking her head in disappointment. She realizes she needs to help, or Bob might not ever make it to the vet.

"Mr. Castle, in my right mind, I do not know if you can take care of this yourself. I just do not feel comfortable. Oh, for goodness sake, I will be by your house tomorrow morning at seven sharp. I will call when done and bring you the bill upon the return of your freshly spayed and fully inoculated Bob."

She laughs as she says the name.

A girl named Bob.

I look down at Bob and then back up to see a retreating Mrs. James humorously shaking her head. How did she accomplish this herculean task single-handedly? Bob looks squeaky clean and calmer than a person who just tried to commit suicide by taking a handful of pot gummies.

Bravo, Mrs. James!

We underestimated each other. I turn my attention to my new furry girlfriend. She smells so much better, just like lavender.

I hope you like that scent, girl.

I could continue to call her Bob, but the perfect name pops into my head, and I immediately give it a shot.

"Hey Alley, are you ready to get out of here?"

She looks at me, her head tilted, but still sitting like a good girl, and I softly pat her on the back.

"You like that name, Alley? You rescued me in an alley. Didn't you, girl? Huh, Alley?"

She gets excited, and I get my first official bark, which startles me a bit, and I almost shit my pants.

I look up to see that all the action inside the entire place has stopped. It was that loud, and everyone was looking at me like I had just farted in church.

"Come on, Alley, let's get out of here before they decide to start burning witches."

That joke didn't go over very well - tough crowd.

Opening the door to leave the air-conditioned pooch palace, I step outside and get blasted by the evening heat. I'm too stubborn to fuck off the rest of the day, and I decide to head to one of those huge pet stores. The sun is setting in a way that looks like a Bob Ross painting, and I take a second to admire it.

After good old Google told me where to go, we parked in the lot and then headed inside the air-conditioned pet superstore. We passed a fancy car parked by the entrance. A driver stood beside it, looking like a menacing, well-dressed statue.

Eyeing my surroundings as we entered, we walked straight to the dog stuff. We start at the toy aisle, and Alley sniffs up a storm, wagging her tail in a way I haven't seen her do before. She looks at me, and I give her an *"it's all yours"* gesture. Tilting her head, she then rushes over to the balls and squeaky toys.

"Get something."

She smells along the rack, sometimes doubling back.

This dog is being thorough.

Alley stops and looks at me again before gently picking up a stuffed pink pig from the bin. She holds it in her mouth delicately and with such care.

Alley bounds back to me, eager and wagging her tail. We walked around the store picking up food, bowls, a nice big dog bed, and a pet first aid kit.

I pushed my loaded cart of goodies up to the register when Alley swayed over to a nearby shelf and started sniffing again. She carefully picks up the box of dog treats between her teeth and brings it back to the cart.

Well, she has it all figured out now.

I pay and then hustle to my Jeep with the new purchases. Upon leaving the store, we passed the fancy car with the gargoyle putting on his tough-guy act once again.

Quick tip: The tougher someone appears, the more sensitive they may actually be. Also, be careful around the quiet ones.

I load our treasure inside the Jeep, and Alley jumps onto the passenger seat. I grab her pig, and she wags her tail excitedly. With a flick of my wrist, I send it flying in her direction. Again, she catches it in the air.

Please teach me your sage Jedi ways.

We pulled out of the spot with Alley beaming, holding her little pink pig in her mouth and enjoying the ride. I'm cruising leisurely to the end of the lane, back toward the store. I see a pretty woman exiting and heading toward the fancy car with the driver holding the door open. Her expression looks like she's calculating a complex assortment of matrix algebra. I'm sure there's a story there, but unfortunately, this town is full of them. We hook a right, exit the lot, and take off down the street.

We both enjoy the open air as we take the highway back. It's summer, so my Jeep's top is off.

I guess you could say I like my Jeep like I like my women - topless.

I turned my gaze toward Alley and observed her. I fell more in love with her, not even realizing I had started to.

Weird.

We arrived back in my building's lot about ten minutes later, and I could tell Alley was happy to be home. She gets out and sniffs around, the pig still in her mouth as I grab our stuff. She pees by the dumpster and then leads the way to our sublevel. I open the door and drag everything inside, throwing my keys on the small table by the door. After filling Alley's food and water bowls to the top, I set them down on the floor. I picked up her treats, noticing how she watched them like a fat kid and the last piece of cake. I move them around and chuckle as her head sways in the same direction as the box. I take one out before placing the box on the shelf and then toss her a cookie, which she catches with ease.

She munches on that and then goes back to bathing Mr. Pig. I put her soft new bed in the bedroom and then kicked back on the couch to chill. I'm just about to turn on the TV when the phone in my pocket buzzes.

"Hello?"

"Code in Foxtrot, One, Niner."

My head instantly goes down.

Fuck!

And I don't want to take this, but I have to.

"Oscar, Delta, Five, Three, Whiskey, Zulu."

I say that slowly into my phone, carefully enunciating each word. I hear a series of clicks before a buzzing tone starts. It lasts about three seconds before someone picks up on the other end.

I hear a familiar but unwelcome voice.

"How's it hanging, dickhead?

"Hey, Jahvey, still alive, huh?"

"Yeah, that's Deputy Director Simbado to you now, shit-head."

Well, they promoted that slimy bastard. I wonder who he fucked over to get that?

Jahvey Simbado is a slippery piece of ball meat with his nasty little fingers and all sorts of weaselly shit. We did some government work for one of the alphabet agencies several times, but he was sloppy and impulsive, and I immediately steered clear of him.

"Anyway, seriously, I need you to take care of something that the agency can't be seen as a part of. I'll pay you so much that you can get plastic surgery to look just like me. Hey, maybe it'll help get you laid."

This guy is a total prickwad.

"Hmm...let me see. I might be able to fit you in between fuck off and suck a bag of dicks! How does that work for you?"

If this douchebag was standing in front of me, I'd throat-punch him.

We banter back and forth for a few minutes, measuring man-meat. We both know just how far to take it before someone blows a gasket.

"You need to say yes to this. I can make your life unbearable with the touch of a button."

In my mind, I see a giant flashing button. *It has "FUCK YOU" written across it and pushing it will ruin your life.* The government doesn't play fair.

I can't figure a way out of this. I have to do it, or my life is going to be a world of shit.

FUCK!

"Well, I really don't have a choice, do I? You know Jahvey, you're a genuine piece of shit. Send it the old way. Oh yeah and tell your mother I won't be able to make it over tonight."

"Fuck y..."

I quickly pushed the call-end button.

I noticed Alley staring at me and then realized I had raised my voice.

"Sorry, I hate dealing with that slimy little troll."

I walk over to her and pet her soft, warm fur.

"We're going on an adventure, girl. Whacha think of that?"

Alley barks once before returning to Mr. Pig, oblivious to the storm that just now started rumbling on the horizon.

Chapter Seven

Sometimes, old school is the best school, and when dealing with the art of subterfuge, the simpler it is, the more it's overlooked and the more effective it becomes. When I was doing spooky things for the gray man, I used to set up dead drops. It's a location pre-selected and used in a conversation to designate the spot. I chose *"Mother"* as I wanted to piss off deputy dipshit, but also because it was still a viable spot.

There was a stone wall by this old church off the 101, about thirty miles from nowhere. The stone in question covered a void where things could be secretly placed. I roll up around sunset, scan the area for a few minutes, looking for a tail, and then park next to the old gray wall. I get out and count the stones, finding the spot with ease even after all this time. I pulled the rock away and grabbed a cheap, plastic, pre-paid phone and then replaced the rock. I turn on the phone and press the only contact in its memory. After a moment, it rang once, and an automated system picked up.

"Code In."

I key my memorized code into the little burner as I climb back into my Jeep. Waiting, I hear soft static modulating in the background, like someone was tuning a radio. A simple tone sounds briefly before a nondescript, recorded male voice reads off a series of numbers. It sounds scripted and narrated straight from the page. There's paper softly rustling in the background.

"Operative, this briefing is considered Taskforce One, Amber Level Classified, and is compartmentalized from the general

NCIS Databases. You must contact Oleg Patinko immediately."

I threw my Jeep in drive and peeled out, already on my way, and the briefing continues.

"He's a white male Russian national, approximately 68 years old, with strong ties as the lead accountant to the Bratve. Specifically, the Vory v Zakone crime group under the leadership of Harriet Fowler, who recently passed away. Intel believes a power shake-up is happening. He's also been a mole for the C.I.A. for two years, and we must keep him in play. The intel we've received from him has saved countless lives."

I'm driving over the bridge, as the recorded message concludes.

"This information was eighteen hours old at the time of your activation. Again, immediately link up with Oleg Patinko at the provided address to receive further instructions. You must now destroy this phone."

"Good luck, Operative."

I pulled my Jeep to the side and transferred the address to my GPS and then tossed the phone into the cold, dark water below the bridge, forever sealing its fate.

I arrived at the Patinko house twenty minutes later and approached a large, modern wooden fence. After a quarter-mile private drive, I'm stopped at a heavy wooden gate with the monitor box mounted on a pillar right by the side of the road. A large digital eye watched me as I pushed the call button.

"Da?"

"Hey, I'm Guy Castle. I was sent over to see your boss by some mutual friends. He's expecting me."

As I wait for the gate to open, I get a funny idea. I push the button again and order the number three, super-sized with a Coke.

Bzzzzzz.

The heavy gate glides on well-oiled wheels as it slides to the side. Entering the private drive, I start to get nervous, seeing the gate closing behind me. It's part of the job, so let's get into character—game face.

I rubbed Alley's ear, my faithful new companion and hope bringing her along was a good idea.

After another stretch of the world's wealthiest driveways, I see the house as I come around a bend. It's lit up all the way around and looks like a modern art installation. Fountains spray from a mirror pool across from the entrance, and the light shimmers as it plays off the water.

I cautiously scan the property and pull up to the house, mentally tagging multiple sentries and dog teams walking overlapping security sweeps. A couple of heavies holding VEPR-12, Magazine-Fed, Semi-Automatic Shotguns guard the door. Like all good little Russian mob muscle cronies, they wear tight black suits, crisp white shirts, and black ties. It seems the higher in the organization you get, the more creative you can be with your outfit.

I park my Jeep and get out. I don't grab my gun from under the seat, as I know they will search me before letting me inside. I lock eyes with the bigger one as I walk up to the door, giving him the *"what's up"* chin wag.

When he returns my greeting with a dead-eyed glare, I laugh and shake my head.

"What's up, tough guy? Your boss is expecting me."

He continues to stare at me as his partner pats me down. Alley stands beside me and growls at the thug when he eyeballs her.

Good girl, Alley.

When Mr. Frisker becomes Mr. Frisky and makes sure I'm not hiding a gun somewhere on my crotch, I wink at him, and he stands up all mad. He then looks at my dog.

"No number three, and dog must stay."

"But I'm hungry, and she's my emotional support dog."

He takes a step toward me threateningly, and Alley growls, exposing her teeth. It freaks out the big, tough guys. Tall, dark, and stupid, allow both of us inside while pretending it was his idea.

We enter a spacious foyer and take in the layout. A formal sitting area is to my right, and what looks like a hallway leads off to the left. The corridor is dark, so I head into the formal sitting room. The room is below the main level and showcases mid-century modern decorations. Windows line the perimeter, and the view takes my breath away.

As I enter the room, I'm amazed by the plush white carpet and the pleasant scent that reminds me of sandalwood. Alley sniffs the air cautiously, and I chuckle when I see her walking across the carpet, her legs raising weirdly as she navigates this new texture. I can tell she's not so sure. Making our way to the other side, we step out onto a large outdoor wrap-around deck.

I can feel the humidity in the warm air tonight, and looking over the city, the lights twinkle like a million little fireflies. I'm sense I'm being watched and turn to find a beautiful woman emerging from the dark.

Although graceful and stunning, she reminded me of a spider in the middle of spinning its web.

"Who are you?"

She speaks with an exotic accent, and as she continues, her vowels roll around like an ice cube on her tongue. Alley sniffs her attentively.

"Why have you come?"

Straightening my shoulders and walking toward her, I extend my hand.

"My name is Guy Castle, and a mutual friend sent me to assist your husband with some protection."

"Ha, my husband needs help with something. And what are you, a magician?"

She looks away in disgust, and I see she's hiding some complex emotions. Alley walks up to her, and the beautiful stranger gently pets her momentarily.

"Well, good luck."

She walks back into the house, Alley watching her leave.

Man, the super-rich are so complicated. It's crazy.

I hear a shuffling sound on the carpet and see Oleg stumbling into the outdoor space, almost tripping on the sliding door frame with his duck foot. Oleg wears a permanent sneer and looks like a bulldog dragging a tire. He heaves himself up to me, his left leg arriving late, compensatory movements from a past injury. He sees me watching and nods with understanding. He reminds me of a James Bond villain, and I give myself a quick slap to refocus.

He really does look like a bulldog.

"Mr. Castle? Good, you made it."

He has a thick Russian accent.

"Do I detect some Georgian, sir?"

I turn to face him. He looks pleasantly surprised at me and nods his head.

"Yes, yes, you are excellent...Proovdasha region. My grand-father had datcha there. All I remember is the cold."

I smile, waiting patiently for him to get to the point. I can tell he's a man who's not accustomed to asking for help. He looks like he's debating before turning to me.

"I have situation that needs special attention. I'm sure you know from our mutual friends that I have problem..."

He pauses dramatically, and Alley perks her ears up. She heard something.

"...problem of delicate nature, and you come highly recommended. I have all the info for you right here."

He handed me a USB stick. I take it and nod my thanks before putting it deep into my pocket.

"You were the principal on the Monroe thing, right?"

At this, I nod, and he nods back as if validating himself. He slowly hobbles over to a sidebar, dragging his fake leg, and pours a drink. As an afterthought, he hands me his glass and pours another. He acts like he's not bothered, but I can tell something spooks him. He's losing his composure. His hand started shaking so nervously that he spilled his drink.

Wait! Is he crying? What the hell?

My soldier-spidey senses kick off, and I instantly scan my environment on alert. I can tell Alley senses something as well. She's looking back inside the room, whining.

Something is very wrong.

Alley stands up and looks around, her eyes darting anxiously before turning to me, alarmed. Gunfire suddenly erupts from the front of the house, and you can hear the doormen return fire with their much deeper-sounding shotguns.

With a violent whoosh and a loud-cracking bang, a rocket slams into the side of the house about fifteen feet from where we're standing. As a result, the front entryway and part of the sitting room are obliterated, and fire catches in the shag carpet. Glass sprays everywhere, slicing through the air, and the immediate area is clouded with a pall of acidic smoke. Sporadic weapon fire pops off as sentries engage the stealthy attackers.

Alley crouched low when the blast happened, and it slid her harmlessly across the floor. Oleg and I weren't as lucky. The concussive wave picks me up and throws me against the expensive glass deck. It craters around me, and I silently bless whoever created safety glass.

Oleg, however, was standing by the bar, which was closest to the blast. It was totally wiped out and now unrecognizable. I see smoldering pieces of wood and bid Oleg...

Dasvidaniya.

Extracting myself from the cratered glass wall and dropping to the floor, I move low towards the shattered remains of the front room. The fire is spreading quickly, and it's starting to climb up the broken walls. Shards of glass litter the ground, sticking into the rug at crazy angles, refracting the orange flickering glow. Sparks are falling like rain, and we need to move.

Alley following low right behind me, we dash through the growing inferno, exiting the blaze through the thickening smoke. We're back into the shattered remains of the front area, which are now hardly recognizable. I hear the sitting room's roof begin to fail and know that I only have seconds before it collapses.

We were about to rush out the door when I remembered the woman, and instinctively changed direction, heading down the dark hallway. I see the demolished remains of my faithful Jeep, my one and only, teetering on its side through the flames as I pass and vow revenge. Mess with me all you want, but that was a collector's Jeep.

Keeping low, Alley rushes in front of me, nose to the ground, entering the igniting hallway. She passes the first doorway, dark and still, heading down to the end of the hall. I looked behind me, noticing the gunfire had stopped. Reaching the end of the hallway, I hear a muffled cough. Alley has disappeared into the room, and I follow to discover her sniffing a closed closet door. The room is rapidly filling with smoke, and I can see that the hallway is now completely engulfed. Tongues of fire are swimming through the smoke as it fills the space, changing the ceiling from white to a thick, murky black.

Yanking the closet doors open, I see a pair of terrified eyes looking back at me from under a pile of blankets. Smoke wafts in, and she coughs again.

"We gotta move!"

I shout out while coughing on the thickening fumes, hurting my throat. I hear the whisking crackle of the approaching fire and know time is critical. I look around and notice a window that, surprisingly, is still unbroken.

Plan B.

I throw a nightstand table through the window, sending it crashing below to vent the room. I'm coughing more and more as I clear the remaining shards of glass from around the frame. Looking out, I judge it's about a 10-foot fall to the sloping ground below.

Wonderful...this is gonna hurt.

I run back and grab Alley, who is struggling with the smoke. She flops over on her side, and I can see she's on the verge of passing out. When our eyes lock, I see her panic. Before we can weigh the options, I pick up Alley and run to the window. Her body pressed into mine, and I rubbed her fur before tossing her out as straight as possible. I watched her body contort and land awkwardly but safely on the ground.

I drop to the floor and scoot back over to the closet. The room is completely enveloped in a rapidly thickening wall of smoke from the flames, so I can't say anything. I pull the frightened woman up and over, hearing a soft "oomph" as her belly lands on my shoulder.

The room is crackling, and I notice the carpet is melting. We pushed off, and I raced to the window. The dense smoke has now banked down almost to the floor. I spin her around so she's closest to the exit and help her climb through safely. When I see her land, I immediately turn to climb out.

Placing a leg out the window, I'm startled to see a phantom emerge from the flames, like a goddamn devil. Vapors swirl around the stranger as he confidently strolls through the smoke and fire toward me.

What the serious fuck?

I notice he's bringing up his weapon, a lethal little submachine gun. I must calculate the instant between jumping through the window and landing. But by doing that, he would be at the window by then, feeding me bad-guy biscuits.

I change direction with a feint, then hurl myself at him, trapping his weapon between our two bodies as we collide. The air is getting so hot I can't breathe it anymore and hold my last precious breath as it rains, embers falling around us. He backs up, and I see he's wearing a full-face breathing mask. The roof has collapsed in the hallway, and I hear the bedroom support beams moan and then crack. With our arms tangled up, I headbutt his mask with all I have. I struck that thing with such force that I felt an electric jolt in the back of my neck, but the effect was worth it. With watering eyes, I see the mask has shattered inward, injuring the surprised hitman and giving me a crucial split second. Using both hands, I grab his jumpsuit and spin him into the burning closet, creating a fireworks-like display of flickering embers. The exertion sends me to the floor, and I don't waste another second. I hear the roof give, and then large pieces of burning wood begin to fall like bombs all around me. Sprinting as my sleeve catches fire and my lungs burn, I dive out the window.

Consequences be damned.

Like a flaming pile of human commando, I hit the ground and roll. Smoke escapes my clothes as I rotate, end over end, kicking up dirt.

It's nothing graceful, but nothing snaps, and I'm not leaking anywhere as I get up, so that's a plus. My clothes are so hot they are releasing vapors, and I pat out a few spot fires on my jacket and pants. I loosen my already-skewed tie and unbutton my scorched shirt. Blood drips from a cut above my eye and down the side of my soot-stained face before creating a Rorschach pattern on my right collar. I dab at it like a dummy and gasp as my fingers clumsily prod the wound, sending a jolt of pain. Alley produces a whine and noses me, sniffing with concern, and I wink at her.

Gonna take a lot more than that to kill me, girl.

I've been watching the window and haven't seen the mystery assailant, and my mind's racing. Who the fuck was that demon? What is happening, who is doing this, and what machinations are at play?

Yeah, I said it, machinations.

I had so many questions and so few answers. I suddenly remember the USB drive that Oleg gave me before the attack. I pull it out of my pocket and check to ensure that it's still okay. It looks fine, and I slide it back in.

As I walk over to the once composed and mysterious woman, she's now on her knees, holding her stilettos, so the heels don't get dirty or break. It's a good thing she had her purse slung across her body when I found her. She seems to be in shock as she watches her shattered house, fire raging throughout. You can hear things crashing and exploding as the ravenous monster consumes everything in its path. The smoldering remains float around us like tears from the dying house.

She doesn't notice that I'm speaking to her, and I lightly touch her arm. Startled, she looks directly at me. Tears cut clean lines down her face, dirty from the smoke, and I'm struck by something in them. Unable to identify it, I helped her up, and we made it to the bottom of the hill, Alley leading the way.

Chapter Eight

I hired an Uber, and we safely escaped the immediate danger. I have the driver take us to my house, but I need information since I don't know what direction to go. The guy gave us a funny look when he picked us up, because we were covered in soot, so I told him we were re-enactors. I can see the wheels turning as he wonders what for, too shy to ask. Alley has taken the front passenger seat and is looking out the window happily.

I shift uncomfortably in the seat, wincing from one of the countless bruises forming over my freshly beaten and burned body. I watch the woman as she looks out the window with unfocused eyes.

"What's your name?"

I have to nudge the shell-shocked beauty to break her out of her stupor.

"Hey, what's your name?"

This time, she looks up and our eyes lock. She has the most beautiful eyes, the color of sea foam. I didn't notice the last time, but who can blame me for that? I can't decide if they are sad, angry or both.

"Svetlana."

"Okay, Svetlana, my name's Guy. You remember? Your husband hired me?"

At this, she nods, and I can tell she's remembering.

"We're heading back to my house to regroup. I promise you I'll keep you safe."

She nods her head and weeps quietly. Her entire world has shattered, and she's now riding in a strange car with a man she doesn't know. I give her an empathetic smile and decide to back off. I look out the window, not even seeing the outside world passing by. My mind is on more pressing things, deadly things.

We arrive ten minutes later in front of my building and exit the car. Alley leads the way as we walk down the stairs, and I can tell Svetlana is a little leery.

I reassured her it was okay and unlocked the door. Alley prances in, and I hold my arm out invitingly for her to follow.

"But it's so dirty."

Looking around, she pouts, refusing to enter. I walk in, closing the door behind me. Through the window, I can still see her shapely legs as she walks back and forth, unsure of what to do. Safety wins over when I hear a shout from someone down the street, and the next thing I know, she's pounding on the door, and I open it.

"Welcome, princess."

She glares at me as she enters, rage steaming from her eyes.

"Don't call me that."

I grin.

"Don't act like one then."

I realize she's surprised. She's accustomed to being in control of the situation; right now she's anything but. She walks around my small man cave, shooting lasers of disdain all over the place as she judges everything. I walk into the kitchen and grab two beers, and then walked back and handed one to her. She holds it awkwardly, like it's a live grenade.

"A beer?"

I look at her as I pop the top of mine and take a big gulp.

Oh no, she's a whiner.

But a gorgeous one at that.

"Can I at least have a glass?"

If she had asked me politely, I would have given her one, but I ignore her and walk into my bedroom to change. After chugging the beer, I place the bottle on my dresser, pull my ripped and singed suit jacket off, and throw it on the floor. As I'm unbuttoning my shirt, I walk over to Alley, who's happily holding Mr. Pig in her mouth. I pat her on the head and then take my shirt off. As I'm pulling my undershirt over my head, I catch Svetlana secretly watching from the kitchen. She blushes and turns away quickly, suddenly interested in my singing fish hanging on the wall. I pull off my ruined pants and put on some sweats. As I'm putting on a t-shirt, I walk out of my room, making sure my eight-pack is exposed long enough to make Svetlana's eyes widen.

"Would you like to clean up?"

I can tell she wants to say something with attitude, but she can only manage a slight nod. I set her up with one of my t-shirts, boxers, and a clean towel, then left her in the bathroom as she looked around, horrified. I close the bedroom door and attempt to figure out what to do next. I saw her unopened beer on the kitchen counter and popped the top on my second for the evening.

I eventually hear the shower start and pull out the USB drive I had taken out of my pocket earlier. I walk over to my laptop sitting on my table and open it. After logging in, I plug the drive into the side and navigate the cursor to open the folder.

Two files were inside: an executable and a standard text document named *"List"*.

I glide the arrow to the executable and click on it. The screen changes, and I see a large picture of Oleg's face as he pushes record on what I assume is his laptop. He sits down, and I see a different Oleg than from the other night. He settles back in his chair and takes a drink from his crystal glass before proceeding dramatically.

"If you are watching this, well, it means that I'm dead. I'm recording, so you will know if that is the case. Don't mourn me, my dear Radnaya. Please remember the times we shared playing in the sun as children."

Why did he give this to me instead of a family member or a close friend? Was he interrupted before completing the setup? Or did he intentionally give it to me? I continue to watch the video, desperate for answers.

"Ah, those times were long ago, and we have both made choices. You will be disappointed, dear sister, but I must tell you the truth. I have made much money doing things I would rather not tell you about. I'm sorry to say I was afraid you would look at me differently if I told you this when I was alive."

He shifts uncomfortably in his chair, taking another sip of his drink and collecting his thoughts.

"In my office where I'm now, you will find a floor safe. It's hidden under a black rug with green edges. The code to get in is your birthday. Inside, you will find a device that you plug into a computer. And when supplied with a special code will transfer a large amount of money into a series of bank accounts, giving you full authorization. Harriet's dog holds the key."

He looks away momentarily and stares off into the distance, lost in thought. Taking another drink, he looks back solemnly at the camera. I see his mask of arrogance and pompous superiority slip for a second.

"I'm so sorry that we drifted apart after the death of our dear mother. I have no excuse, and I respect you too much to lie.

While I was a bastard in life, please remember me as your innocent little brother chasing grasshoppers with you again in the field."

He holds his hand to his mouth, kisses it and touches the screen.

"Dasvidaniya."

The video ends with a close-up shot of Oleg's face frozen the moment he stopped recording.

Well, that was depressing.

I move the arrow over to the list.doc and click. I see columns of numbers. Then, looking closer, I notice some lines that are just numbers, while others are numbers and letters, and the more I scroll down the page, I see complete words. I know this is important, but it's over my head, and I will need to bring in some help. I know the perfect person. As I minimize the list.doc, I see Oleg's big face again and start chuckling.

I'm getting ready to call my brainy friend when Svetlana exits my room and slinks toward me with a deviously innocent smile. I had given her sweats, a shirt, and boxers; the whole nine, and here she comes strutting in wearing only my t-shirt. It's long enough to cover all the good stuff, and I wonder if she's paying me back from earlier. My mind turns to naughtier things, but I play it off like I don't notice.

It takes work.

Her hand grazes mine as I pass right by, attempting to get myself a glass of water. I try to think of something else, anything else. She's stunning and smells incredibly fresh. While pouring my water, I hear her gasp. I look back and catch her standing in front of my open laptop. She can't take her eyes off the frozen screen with the picture of Oleg, who's staring right back at her.

I rushed over and closed it, but the damage was already done. Where she was confident and in control only moments before, her demeanor had completely changed. Her shoulders start to shake and curl inward as she cries. This has been a rough night. I go to the kitchen, grab a bottle of the hard stuff and walk back to her, guiding her onto the couch. As she sits, I catch a glimpse of sexy red lace peeking out from under the shirt hemline and then hand her a blanket hesitantly. She pulls it over her long, smooth legs, and I sit next to her, taking a pull from the bottle. I pass it to her, and she takes a swig. I'm quiet, giving her the space to talk. We sit like this for a few minutes, passing the bottle back and forth until she speaks.

"I never loved him."

I'm still trying to determine who she's talking to. Maybe herself, so I stay quiet.

"Oleg was a lot of things, but believe it or not, he was incredibly kind to me...until he wasn't."

She looks down at the bottle swirling the brown liquid inside. She looks at me, and I see a depth of grief that I would not have suspected. As she takes another drink, I can tell the warm liquor is taking effect. She hands me back the bottle, and the blanket shifts, revealing more red lace. She catches me staring.

Oops.

"You saved me."

Svetlana looks at me with pleading eyes and the blanket falls to the floor, forming a perfect puddle of softness and a barrier from the worn carpet below. As she intentionally stretches, her t-shirt rides up, revealing an overwhelming amount of sheer silk and red lace. She leans toward me, and I take that as an invitation to explore her nether regions.

But not quite yet.

You see, I like to take my time, and I would never take advantage of a grieving woman. But the thing is, I'm loving what I'm seeing, and what harm would it do anyway? She made the first move.

I lean toward her, softly grabbing her by the shoulders, pulling her body against mine. I kiss her as my hands graze slowly over her curves. She shadows my moves, and it doesn't take long before her hand is between her legs.

I guess I'll shadow her now.

I lower my hand and begin moving it closer to the delicate fabric, her legs part, exposing her most sensitive spot. I play with her for a while before I slip my finger under the edge of her panties and feel her wetness and warmth. She thrusts her hips toward my hand, begging to be taken, but I tease her by pulling my finger out and smoothly gliding it down her thigh, then back up with two fingers inching closer to the edge.

Wait! Stop! What the hell am I doing?

I froze up for a second, pulled my hand away, and then backed off. Svetlana looked at me in shock. I know what she was thinking. How can anyone resist me?

Be professional and stay focused.

While I don't think she was responsible for the incident tonight at the house, she knows more than she's letting on. We end up talking for a while longer, but when fatigue overtakes her, I cover her up on the couch, then leave.

I would give her my bed, but that's not a good idea, and I know it.

I head into the bedroom, Alley following me with a soggy Mr. Pig in her mouth. As I lay my head on my pillow, my mind refuses to stop racing. But soon, exhaustion wins again, and I slip into the black.

Chapter Nine

I awake and feel the bruises and burns from the night before, groaning as I sit up in bed. I tossed and turned all night, fighting with the sandman, and he finally won in the early morning. I hate it when I don't have all the pieces for a puzzle, and right now, I have only completed a flimsy frame. I look over to say hi to Alley and am surprised she's not in bed. I turn to look at the clock and realize Mrs. James will arrive in a few minutes to pick her up. I momentarily stretch my poor body as I think about my crazy life choices. I walk out of my bedroom and over to the blessed coffee pot.

I wonder how she slept.

"Hey, time to get up."

I say this as nicely as I can. I hate being woken up. I walk over to nudge Svetlana, seeing Alley by the door, and am startled to see she's not there. I see the blanket tossed across the cushions and spot the t-shirt she was wearing crumpled on top. I notice her pillow had a dent, so I gently put my hand up to it, feeling for warmth and detecting it slightly.

Ok, that means she slept here and only left recently.

Alley looks at me with a "yup" expression, and I curse my life silently. This dame is going to be the death of me. Fuck it, I have always lived a life worth dying for. Ok, adventure, I'm coming; please give me a second. I dash into my room, dressing quickly as I slam my cup of coffee.

Priorities.

I have a hunch I know where she's going—back to her house.

There's a knock on the door, and it's Mrs. James. She's happy, picking up Alley as if they were having a sleepover. She cracks me up. What a wonderful woman. I hired an Uber and tried not to yell at the lovely old lady who arrived late. I need to get there fast, and while she's going the speed limit, she keeps trying to engage me in conversation.

Sheesh lady, give a guy a chance to think, will ya?

My irritated driver dropped me off nine minutes later, and I heard her mumble some smart-ass remark as I was getting out.

I agree lady, I am a rude motherfucker.

I hop the gate and sprint up the long, twisting road toward the mansion. As I get close, I veer off to the right and approach the place, walking along the edge of the front area. The scent of pine is strong, and I see some branches that have been snapped off and bullet holes in the trunk. Everywhere, I see scattered bark chips and empty shell casings. The once beautiful castle-like house is now a giant crater of black amorphous shapes sticking out at crazy angles like ribs from last night's feast. The estate was a chaotic display of ruin. From across the way, I spot Svetlana on her hands and knees, clumsily crawling around on the floor, picking through the debris.

God damn nuisance!

I'm about to exit my hide and call out, but my eye catches movement to the left. I see an enormous figure sneaking up from around the other side. I watch him as he pulls a gun out. When I notice him easily attaching a long silencer to the end, I realize whoever is holding that weapon knows how to use it. I see his calculated movements as he attempts to get a better angle, which is good for me, as this will bring him closer. I look in my immediate area for a weapon. Anything can be a weapon in a pinch if enough violence is provided. I settle on a large stone, bummed at my limited options.

I guess I am a goddamn caveman. My exes will agree.

He's arcing closer, gun raised, poised to take the shot when he lines up to me momentarily. This is the assassin's first and last big mistake. He was so focused on the target that he stopped paying attention to his peripherals. Timing my ambush, I fly out of his blind spot, cracking him in the head with the rock. He had little time to react as I did it rapidly and as silently as possible. With a sickening crunch, the dead man drops to the ground. I snatch up his gun and then drag his crumpled, lifeless body into the trees.

One down. What's next?

I'm pretty deadly, but if you put any weapon in my hand, I turn lethal in a flash. While fuckboys were in the bars bragging about what they did the night before, trying to be all badass, I was honing my skills in every shit hole around this fucked up world. I tuck the weapon behind me in my belt and approach Svetlana as quietly as possible.

What the hell is she up to?

She's no longer crawling and scavenging; now, she's crouched down like a catcher but still messing with something on the floor. She's so absorbed in whatever she's searching for that she hasn't noticed me or the little rock and roll that just went down. She pulls up something metal, and I catch her red-handed.

"Morning, princess. How did you sleep?"

She's so startled she loses her balance and falls over. Turning to look at me, she starts to say something but freezes up, and not a single word comes out. Walking up to her, I analyze the thing in her hand and get an icy shiver running through my body. It looks like a crypto-locker. Although I have never seen one before, I have a nerd friend who fills me in on all the latest weird and tech. Supposedly, if you have the authentication code, it routes multiple large fund crypto accounts into one giant money transfer that's used for transactions ten digits and over sending it to the account of the authenticator's choosing.

"Whacha got there?"

I love playing country dumb.

"These are just memories and important papers backed up for protection."

I know she's lying, and I mentally debate if I should call her out, but then decide that this is not the time. We need to get the fuck out of here, most ricky tick.

So, being the gentleman I am, I extend my arm and offer Svetlana a hand. She grabs ahold, and helping her to her feet, we climb out of the wreckage and bid farewell to the detritus of her former life. What a waste. I won't mention anything about the attempt on her life, either. I need her to focus; she doesn't seem like the type that can juggle multiple life events simultaneously.

We return to the main road, and I call for another ride. In complete silence, we stand on the side of the road, waiting for the car to arrive. I am trying to figure this chick out. I can tell she's lost in thought, and I notice her tucking her hair back behind her ear on the right side. I'm surprised I don't see any emotion on her face.

But who am I to judge?

A random driver comes to pick us up, and after an uneventful ride, I have him drop us off downtown. We need to get lost in the crowd. The more people around us, the better. There is safety in numbers, literally. We walk around for a while, and Svetlana buys an overpriced sugar coffee from one of those trendy joints. We sit at one of the storefront tables, and as she drinks it, she reluctantly hands me the small metal drive after I ask for it, then I quickly slip it into my backpack.

Photos and memories, my ass!

I need to figure out what to do next, and right away.

I'm pondering that when I notice a woman eyeballing us from a nearby table. I constantly analyze people's eyes because they are the hardest thing to disguise. Hers are complex and much too hard for the soccer mom I see her trying to be.

How did they find us?

I look at Svetlana as she drinks her coffee, and it clicks. They must have some crazy tech tracking her credit card transactions.

"Hey, let's get out of here."

We exit the trendy spot and hook a left. We're downtown, and I scan the businesses looking for options. I see art galleries, a bank, a pop-up immersive experience and a little corner grocery store. I hear they call them bodegas on the East Coast.

I head across the street toward the experience, an immersive walkthrough of history's most incredible movie scenes. We enter the building and buy two tickets. I feel the heat from the woman walking up behind us as we turn to enter. She's calculating her odds and doesn't like the total.

We walk into a room that is a brightly lit yellow brick road with fake trees on either side. Dopey music plays as a pair of actors dance around. I fly past them, trying to get more distance between the woman assassin and us. I see her enter the room, and we slip out the other door. I look around for an ambush spot. The surroundings are darker here, and the light is creating kaleidoscopic shades of blue on the artificial water surrounding us. A prop pirate boat is in front of us, and we dart up the short ladder. Jaunty music plays from hidden speakers, extolling the joys of yo-ho-hoeing.

I turn around and kneel, lining my now-drawn weapon at the door. It slowly opens, and the woman smoothly slips through the opening. We fire at each other multiple times as she does this, missing each other by centimeters. By this time, Svetlana had reached the other door and entered the next room. She's panicking and is starting to move further away from me. I have an idea: turning around, I sprint to the door and slide through right before it closes.

This new room strobes in different light patterns as some weird sci-fi music plays. An actor in a robot suit shuffles out of a side door and starts to do his thing. Running past him, I accidentally knock him into the wall beside the door.

"Hey!"

I look behind me and see the woman slide into the room. She sees me racing through the door and takes chase. As I clear the opening, I slam my back to the wall and raise my gun. The chase was too much for her to resist, and she makes a fatal mistake. She bursts through the doors, assuming I am still running ahead.

Pwep, Pwep, Pwep

I hit her with all three rounds I fired. The first two land center mass and the third catches her at the base of the neck.

Instant lights out.

The room is horror-themed, and she slides into the side of a fake gravestone, knocking over a fog machine. She kind of looks like her corpse belongs as part of the scene, and I wonder how long it will take before someone realizes that she is a real body. I catch up with Svetlana as she hits the exit door, and we both squint as the bright light blinds us. I grab her and pull her to my side before she can run again. After a moment, she relaxes, and we continue to walk that way. We are just two lovers out enjoying the wonderful day. We need to get off the street right now, and I decide to return to my place. We duck into a side alley, and I call for a rideshare.

There is nothing to see here.

After a tense couple of minutes, the world's dirtiest car pulls up. The driver looks like a scruffy hippy, and he gives me the hang loose hand sign as we enter his cluttered vehicle. He wears a golf hat and his shaggy, curly hair spills from around the edges. The more I look at him, the more he reminds me of Shaggy from that old Scooby Doo cartoon.

Zoiks Scoobs!

He had earphones in and grooved to the music in the front seat as he navigated the busy streets. I look at Svetlana, and as she starts to speak, I discreetly shake my head when I see the driver's eyes in the rearview mirror.

Wait.

When I see she understands the signal, I sent with my eyes; I revert them to the driver. Svetlana looks back at me with a puzzled expression, and I see the guy return to bopping around. Is that a coincidence?

Better safe than sorry.

Chapter Ten

We arrive at my apartment and bid our suspicious driver au revoir. He putters away as we enter my underground lair. Svetlana makes judgy noises and walks around carefully, like she could catch a disease if she touches anything. How much of this has been programmed into her by social media? I try to ignore it as I get ready to call my friend about the mysterious list, but she keeps ramping it up. I have a mental image of her screaming nonstop in my ear if I keep pretending not to notice, so I give in and turn to her.

"What?"

"I should not be here. I'm accustomed to much better, and the stress is not good for me or my skin."

I look at her and see a woman whose most significant stressors are choosing between shopping at Gucci or Chanel or going to the day spa, but once again, who am I to judge?

"What's wrong with my place?"

She points around, stuttering something strange before ending up near the couch.

"I woke up on that filthy thing this morning and was worried I had bugs!"

How ironic this statement will become later.

I can't help myself but crack a smile. I chuckle a bit as I shake my head.

This chick has no clue.

"You have no bottled water. My Wi-Fi signal is non-existent, and you live below the street! What if it rains?"

Really? How do I teach civil and building engineering to this toddler? I need her calm and contained while I deal with this threat.

"Ok, princess."

At this, I get the fiery eyes.

Fuck her.

"Let's go. We'll get a nice hotel somewhere where you can spa and eat room service to your spoiled little heart's content."

I thought I would get an angry reaction from her, but she's nodding her head enthusiastically. She heard spa and room service, and her mouth started watering. I go into the bedroom, throw some clothes in my backpack, and see the crypto-locker again. Then, I come out to find her messing with my laptop and trying to turn it on. I make a noise and act like I'm just coming out of the room, curious about what I saw. I cross over to the laptop and put it in my backpack, and then I remember I need to call my friend. We have been old friends since childhood, and she's one of the most intelligent and talented people I know. I push her contact button and wait as it rings.

"Hello?"

"What's up, Corn Flakes?"

We created code names as kids, and they have followed us ever since. We couldn't think of suitable names then, so we used our favorite cereal.

"Trix?"

"One and only. How's things?"

"Slow. Why you got something?"

"I think so, but I need your stupidity to make sure."

"Ha...fuck you! Where are we meeting?"

I glance at Svetlana.

"The Four Seasons. Meet us in an hour, and make sure you are not being followed."

"Gotcha."

She hangs up.

I look at Svetlana, and I can tell she's happy with my choice of hotel. We leave, and I have us walk a few blocks to ensure we don't get Shaggy again and use a different company altogether to get another car. I create some distance.

Little did we know whoever was coming after us already knew where we were going, as they had bugged my apartment while we were gone earlier that same day.

We're hanging out on the sidewalk in clear sight, and I'm nervous. A beige minivan pulls around the corner, and I silently pray for it to pass us by, but it stops. I slide the door open and see a stocky older woman with a bulbous nose, rosacea, and curlers in her hair. She's wearing pom-pom earrings and a shell necklace. As she spins her seat toward us, I couldn't help but notice her feet. She had on tube socks and the most humongous-sized rubber shoes imaginable. They were such an odd shape that they threw me off for a second. She wore green and yellow plaid Bermuda shorts, a thick black leather belt and a fanny pack. To me, it looked as if she was wearing someone else's clothing. Then she begins speaking with a heavy Wisconsin accent and a startling lisp.

"Golly gee willikers, hop on in! You are my very first riders ever!"

Not another weirdo!

We climb into her taupe mommy-mover, and she turns around and beams, displaying a set of very loose dentures.

Clickety-clack.

"Welcome. I'm doing this for extra money after my poor Gerald died. Bless his heart."

Oh no, please stop.

She turns back around, talking constantly, and gently pulls away from the curb.

What is with my luck and drivers lately? Sheesh!

"Gerald always liked to be handy, and he was cleaning out the leaves on a ladder. Poor Gerald's feet were always so sweaty when he was nervous, and who really super-duper-like hated heights, but I think he was secretly proud to climb that far up the ladder. Well, he was wearing his favorite Croc shoes. Do you know them? Those cute rubber Croc shoes. Well, just in case you don't, looky-looky here! I'm wearing them now. Well, let me get back to my dear, sweet GerBear. Wouldn't you know it? His foot slipped right out of the Croc shoe, and he broke his neck! My Gerald was always so clumsy; that is one of the first things that attracted me to him. Oh, silly me. My name is Marge, by the way. Marge Belfoin! Nice to meet you. Oh, how I prattle. I'm always saying to myself, come now, Marge! But I have been pretty lonely since, my dear Gerald..."

She drones on and on, talking for both of us. I wonder how Gerald took it and how much of his slip was an accident. We take twenty minutes to get to the hotel, with Marge talking the entire time. As we leave Marge and exit the car, she continues to speak faster and faster until I slam the door.

Good luck with the ride-share thing, Marge. You should start a podcast.

We walk into the brightly lit reception area and up to the expensive-looking counter. An excessively pleasant young twenty-something checks us in. She's overly perky and can't stop extolling the many things to do while on the property. I look at Svetlana and see she's hanging on to every word.

They are about the same age and look like they are both riding the same crazy train. Their eyes sparkle as they talk about the towels.

This chick craves luxury like a vampire craves blood.

I eventually break them up and get us an upper-level California suite, and we head for our room. It's weird to check into a hotel with just a backpack between us, but what can you do? We enter the upscale suite, and Svetlana exhales like she has been holding her breath this whole time. She pushes past me and disappears around the corner into the bedroom. I walk straight in and continue down the little hallway into the main TV area. The room is decorated in a modern, clean style, and I swear I can see at least eight different shades of white as I look around. Everything is white, mixed with rich dark wood. I pull open the little mini-fridge and pull out a tiny bottle of Jack. I crack it and take a sip, moving to the balcony to enjoy the view.

After a few minutes, I go back in and hear the shower running. I'm sure Svetlana is scrubbing the shame of my place off her bougie frame. I enter the bedroom and put one of my bank cards on the dresser. I then go to the bathroom door and knock.

"Hey. I left my card on the dresser for if you need anything. Remember not to use your cards, or we will have to leave."

I hear her make an exasperated noise.

"Yes, yes, I know. I stay like good little puppy until you return."

I can't tell if she's joking or if it's just a weird Russian analogy. I decide not to give a shit and head to my backpack, removing the crypto-locker. Walking over to the room safe in the closet, I lock it, making the code 1996.

Soon after, I kick up my feet on the couch. I reach behind and pick up the room phone, which rings the front desk automatically. I order some clothing catalogs to be sent up so Svetlana can get some new clothes. That should keep her pinned down for at least a little while. I look at my watch, and it's still about fifteen minutes until my old friend Aria, or as I like to call her, Cornflakes, arrives. I'm trying to figure out what the list has to do with Oleg's weird, sorry video, and I suddenly sit up.

No. It can't be.

I grab my laptop and return to the desk, which is also white. I plug in my old geek pad and insert the jump drive. I open the text.doc and sit back, looking at the column of numbers. Could these be bank accounts, crypto accounts, and wallets? How much money am I looking at here? I'm so glad I called Aria.

A chill runs down my spine as I realize the high stakes involved in this new game that I now find myself in.

Chapter Eleven

Aria Medahlia-Storm is a legit genius with an IQ that would make Einstein blush. Guy had called back with the room number, and she was leaving. However, at this moment, she can't find her keys. She tries to keep things where they are supposed to be, but sometimes she forgets and sometimes thinks of a better spot. Aria usually gets distracted as big thoughts collide, constantly examining and reevaluating every detail. She finds them under a thick spread of papers on relativistic physics as applied to computer science.

Oh, that's where that went, huh?

She grabs her keys and stops to look in the mirror on her way out. She checks her hair, brushing her even bangs straight before grabbing her coat and heading to her car. Getting into her silver Prius, she fastens her seatbelt. She realizes her keys are not in her hands and pulls them out of her pants pocket after a panicked second of patting and searching.

While driving, she breaks out of her daydream coma and realizes she's been driving in silence. As she turns on the radio, she scans through the different stations. She understands how to use Bluetooth to connect her phone and play her downloaded songs, but she finds the unpredictability of scanning stations both old-school and exciting. She looks down at the radio and doesn't notice the brightly colored vehicle approaching quickly behind her. The windows are very dark, and you can't see through them. When she looked up, it was too late, and the red car was level with her back quarter panel. The driver nudges her hard and at an angle, spinning her out of control. Dirt and debris are spitting out as Aria's Prius is violently sent whirling around in a circle, shattering plastic and glass, before she slams into the cement wall of an underpass. The collision sends her head smashing into her front airbag, and Aria blacks out for a moment. Her crumpled car's metal is ticking from the heat as fluids spill over the debris-strewn street. The red car pulls to a stop next to the wreck, and a tall man wearing a skin-tight wetsuit leaps out. He jumps on the hood violently, kicking the front windshield in. He uses a seatbelt cutter to slice her belt quickly and is pulling her out of her seat through the window when Aria comes to. Her head hurts, and she's feeling sick, but she fights anyway. Getting her hand under his mask, she scratches the tall man's face before he hits her with a stun gun and angrily pulls her unconscious form through the window. He unceremoniously dumped her into the trunk of his car before checking his bleeding face. She lays before him, her crumpled form a tangle of limbs and hair.

"Bitch! Now, I'm going to make it slow."

Grumbling, he slams the trunk, dabbing at his scratched face, gets in his car, and is gone before the first emergency vehicle arrives. Aria wakes in a panic as the car begins to move. Her anxiety is spiking, as she can't see anything. She's on the verge of becoming hysterical when she sees a crack of light by what must be one of the turn lights. She focuses on the light, willing herself to calm down and think of a way to get out of here. She looks around, but the trunk only contains random insignificant items and a couple of used pucks of surfer wax. She goes back to her tiny light and focuses on it like a lifejacket in a storm, her mind raging with anxiety. She calms down, but she has never enjoyed being in tight spaces.

No, I can't. I need to get out, out, get out, get.

Hyperventilating in the tight confines of the hot trunk, Aria succumbs and slips into unconsciousness, the panic dragging her under.

When she regains consciousness, Aria realizes she's sitting up. She gradually opens her eyes, feeling like they have sandbags attached. Her head throbs and the lights seem too bright. A hard slap across the face leaves her ears ringing. She slowly raises her eyes, blood dripping from her split lip. She glares at this tall fuck, wishing him death. That pissed her off, and she needed to control this situation the best she could right now. She needed to stall. He comes in for another slap, and she spits blood all over him, then begins to laugh, as he jumps back, her blood now all over the front of him.

"Crazy bitch, what's so funny?"

He glares, walking back up to her.

"Crime scene forensics, motherfucker. My DNA is all over you and this shithole where you probably fuck all your bitchboys wishing you were a real man."

At this, he looks around, suddenly unsure, and she can see his wheels turning.

"Let me go right now; this doesn't need to get ugly."

"Bitch, you are in no position to be offering deals...don't you realize how fucked you are?"

She smirks at him with a chilling expression as she cocks her head to the side a little, as if judging him, before shaking her head with a hint of sorrow.

"Nah, you are too stupid. I'm already talking to a dead man. If you have a mama, I'd call her and say goodbye."

"Shut up, bitch."

He's spooked.

She laughs again and yells at him as he rushes away.

"You're already a ghost, motherfucker!"

About fifteen minutes later, the roll-up doors rise, and a slick Cadillac rolls in like an old-school gangster. It parks, and four big thugs get out, adjusting their guns. The last to get out is a huge individual carting a machete. As he exits, the car shifts back up, lumbering to the others as they walk toward the skinny man. He's sitting on a stack of tires, looking worried, dabbing at a scratch across his face. He is relieved to see backup and jumps up.

"She's back here. I think she's crazy...just saying."

He makes a weird hand gesture, while showing Aria's location. The muscle moves past him without even a "fuck you." The pecking order is being established, and he knows where he falls...all the way to the bottom. They enter the room where Aria is and then spread out like bad guy-themed decor. The mouthpiece for the world's worst boy band glares at her.

"My boss is on the way. I would think long and hard about cooperating. You might still make it out of this alive."

He smiles broadly, but his eyes are still hard and full of menace.

Liar!

Aria says nothing and instead looks down at her lap. She won't give these motherfuckers any satisfaction from seeing her scared. She divides whole numbers in her mind, constantly doubling the equations.

"Damn! Little Blanca here is tough! Okay, have it your way."

Before she knows it, she has a bag over her head. As soon as she looks down, she immediately tenses up and is about to scream, but then she notices she can see from around the edge of the bottom. She can see her lap and the dirty cement floor. She concentrates on these details as she waits, knowing someone will be here soon. Guy has never let her down, and her sister would kickbox the devil himself to protect her. Her "twin senses" tell her that help is on the way and will be there soon.

Chapter Twelve

When Arias's car crashed into the wall, her twin sister Avery was returning to their two-bedroom apartment. Coming from a sparring session at her dojo, she tosses her gym bag down on the couch as she passes by. She grabs a water bottle from their fridge and downs half of it in a greedy rush. She walks back into the main area, looking around for her twin.

"Aria?"

Her phone rings out of the blue, and she answers, still looking around.

"Hello?"

"Hey Avery, it's Guy. Is your sister there by chance? We had a meeting, and she's now a half hour late, which, as you know, is not like her."

She hears a slight panic in his voice that makes her mad.

"You always drag her into things, and she gets hurt, and you wring your hands. Stay away from my sister, Guy. I have always thought you were, and you still are, bad news."

"Come on, Avery, you have never given me a chance. I'm not that same kid running wild anymore."

"No, you're even worse!"

She takes a deep breath. If her sister is missing, she will need this clown's help.

"Where are you? I will come to you."

"We're at the Four Seasons. Room 503. Thank..."

She hangs up, not interested in anything else he says.

Avery arrives at the hotel twenty minutes later and knocks impatiently. I meet her at the door, head inside, and go down the hall. We sit on either end of the couch as far from each other as possible. The tension in the room could be cut with a knife, but it would break it. I clear my throat.

"So, I know where she is, a location anyway. There's a problem, though. I'm on a job right now, and they know what I look like."

At this, she gives me the no-shit look.

"Right, so they know my name, and I want to try to get her without them getting spooked. Would you b..."

"Yes Motherfucker, let's go!"

She doesn't even let me finish.

I lean back a little at this and shake my head. I have never liked the distance between Avery and myself. Why is it common for siblings to feel the need to pick a side? I was an only child and would never understand their complex interpersonal relationships. We were all friends once.

I stood up and retrieved my backpack, setting it on the desk. I pulled a small case from inside and walked over to Avery. She stands as I open the lid, revealing a thin, translucent dot.

"This is a passive tracker, and an active audio surveillance device. I can hear everything and always know where you are up to a meter."

I use my fingertip to press the little dot and then draw it up carefully. I part Avery's hair almost intimately and push my fingertip to her scalp. I run my fingers through her long black hair, skillfully placing and smoothing the hair over the powerful little device. Avery realizes her eyes are closed, her mouth open, and quickly backs up a pace, clearly confused by the conflicting feelings she just had. I smile sadly at her before picking my phone up from the white coffee table.

I open an app and walk back to her, placing the phone close to where I had put the bug. A soft tone sounds as the device links. I look at the screen, check, and then nod before turning my phone off and placing it in my back pocket.

"How do you know where my sister is?"

The confusion is obvious on her face.

"I uh, I...well, I put a passive tracker on the earrings I gave her for Christmas a few years back."

When she gives me the stalker look and gets mad again, I quickly cut her off.

"It's not like that, and you know it. I know you don't like me, but come on? The nature of this business is always unstable, and I watch out for my own!"

"Clearly!"

She walks past me and to the door.

That stung.

"Text me the address. I will get my sister. She's my family! Stay away from us before your bullshit spills over, and we all suffer the collateral damage!"

She slams the door with that, and I'm rooted to the floor.

Was she right? What am I doing? Why?

Then, I remember the first mission I did for the shadow agency that I can't seem to escape, and now I again find myself working for them. A poor old lady had made a bad financial move with a ruthless gang and could not repay the inflated interest. Little did the gang know, but that old lady was the grandmother of a team guy we lost a few years back. We always take care of our own. Nothing I did that day was anything other than cleaning up some trash and re-establishing some order in this topsy-turvy life. I'm distracted as I leave the room, yelling for Svetlana to stay there.

I left without hearing her response. Hopefully, she caught what I said.

Chapter Thirteen

Avery loves to ride her motorcycle and would enjoy it at any other time, but worry distracts her mind. Aria is all she has; she can't imagine a life without her. She's making good time, weaving around the cars, racing to the spot Guy pinged on her map.

After this, we'll settle up. Never again!

She finds the area and parks her bike about a block away. Approaching on foot and unable to shake the foreboding she feels, she creeps closer to the old meat processing facility where her sister is. It's closed now and won't reopen till the morning.

Oh, what violent dances happen in the dark while the innocent sleep.

Avery is creeping up to the building when one of the hired thugs emerges from the dark behind her. The man surprises her from behind in the dark and knocks her unconscious with a stun baton. The thug throws her over his shoulder like a sack of potatoes and walks back into the dark, bringing her to the building like a spider to its web.

She's lying on the ground beside a chair when she regains consciousness. Avery looks up and sees her sister in the chair next to it. They had tied up Aria and put a bag over her head. Her chest is rising and falling rapidly, clearly in a state of panic.

"R?"

Avery croaks out, and at this, Aria turns her head frantically, trying to place the sound.

"V? Get me out of here."

Aria cries, struggling against the ropes that bind her. Seeing her sister hurt, panicked, and crying, Avery feels like someone poured gasoline into the fire of her soul. Strength, which she did not think she had, surges through her body, and she rises like the warrior she is. Upon returning with a rope, the moron is startled to see her standing. He has one ear and a scar from his forehead to his cheek. His eye twitches when he gets angry, and it blinks like crazy.

Avery tilts her head to the side, cracking her neck as she raises her fists and spreads her legs shoulder-width apart. She's settling into her classic stance when the thug drops the rope and charges her. This time, he doesn't have the stun baton and grossly overestimates his situation. Avery catches his first wildly flung punch and redirects all his energy forward, launching the startled hood right past her. He lands painfully, awkwardly sprawled out on the floor, then slowly rises on shaky legs, calling for help. Aria panics and struggles against her binds in the background as Avery turns and smiles viciously at the surprised, tough guy. This time, he walks slower and more calculated towards her. He thinks he has a more extended reach. She reads this and lands a spinning roundhouse, connecting the ball of her foot with the man's temple.

Lights out, scumbag.

The jerk crumples where he stands, and his head hits the cement with a dull thud. Avery is fighting more on reactions and emotions right now, and the lack of spatial awareness lets the two goons behind her sneak up. One wears a blue shirt, and the other dons a leather strap on his right wrist. Blue shirt grabs Avery from behind, and he instantly flies over her shoulder. While she has this guy, the other lands a powerful punch to the side of her head, rocking her. She stumbles to the left, fighting off the flash from the comic book stars she sees.

A tall, skinny man in a wetsuit unexpectedly arrives at her side. He throws a punch but is so scared there is no actual power or commitment behind it. It glances off Avery's jaw, and she traps his arm there, twisting her body violently to the side while simultaneously kicking out, striking the man's knee. The effect is apocalyptic to the tall drink of dank shit-water. She aggressively rips his elbow and shoulder out of the socket while simultaneously shattering his knee from the side.

He will never walk normally again, but that's the least of his concerns. As he falls, he joins Aria in screaming. Avery turns and stomps hard on the side of his skull. With a wet crack, he's silenced, and he convulses violently like a toy that's short-circuiting, arms flopping, legs kicking. As she steps over the limp mess of neoprene, the other thug squares up. They punch, kick, duck, and weave momentarily, the skilled fighters playing a lethal game of chess. Scuba Steve stops flopping, but then Blue Shirt joins in.

It's just not fair.

To Avery's credit, she is doing better than most of the men and even getting in a few good hits when a humongous thug plods his way into the room. His body is massive, and he has a baby face, red cheeks, and all. His machete rests proudly on his shoulder.

As she deflects a punch from Blue Shirt, it turns her toward the giant we will call Tiny, just for the hell of it. He kicks out, striking her like an enormous tree trunk hit her. The violent change of direction makes Avery dizzy, and she can't block the machete as it sweeps down, slicing across her beautiful face. To her, it feels like a dull thud, followed by cold and then incredible pain that continues to grow as the reality of what had just happened sinks in. Tears fill her eyes as she feels the deep groove on her forever blind eye.

My face! My eye! Oh my god, the blood.

Her hands cover her destroyed face as her warm lifeblood flows alarmingly fast through her fingers. She doesn't even register the punch that knocks her out.

Silence.

***

There was silence, except for the sound of a body being dragged and a latch opening. The laughter of the thugs grew fainter as they moved farther away. The last noise was the clang of the door being closed, then locked.

Guy had been monitoring all this as he urgently called for a ride. Anxiously waiting near the curb for his rideshare, hand to his ear listening, he's losing his patience. Taking a step closer to the street, he sees a man starting his motorcycle and making adjustments to his helmet. While pacing, an idea suddenly pops into his head, motivating his next move.

Weighing the odds for half a second, he rushes over to the man who is about ready to take off and catches him off guard. Guy knocks the man off the bike, sending him spinning and landing on his ass. Guy jumps on the man's motorcycle and speeds off down the street yelling an *"I'm sorry"* over his shoulder. He's beating himself up for involving the Storm Sisters, straining to hear anything, and covering the earbud with his hand.

One more reason I like to work alone. No one else can get hurt because of me. I must save them. Now!

I panic as snow and fire drift into my overtaxed mind. Mentally, I bore down, pushing that thought back into the frosty box it had escaped from. I hit a pothole and temporarily lost control of the bike. I need to focus on the twins, their safety, their lives. I need to focus on the road before I kill myself, abandoning the twins forever. I shake my head, eliminating the intrusive thoughts that could potentially destroy my mental well-being forever.

It's late, and as I park the bike, I notice it's quiet and there's no activity. This part of the city sleeps at night, oblivious to the invisible war around them. I hop off the bike and place a gun under my belt behind my back and the knife in my jacket pocket. I look around once more to be sure.

All clear. Now let's get this done.

I sneak along the edge of the wall, hidden in the shadow. I feel the reassuring press of the weapon behind my back, and my palms sweat. Approaching cautiously, I readjust the knife. When I see the building, I sit in the shadows for a moment and study my surroundings. There are no city cameras, and none of the buildings are lit up. My eyes pick up subtle movement across the street, and I see a thug in a blue shirt. He's hiding in the dark but shifting around. He's rubbing his shoulder, possibly because of an injury. After another moment of observation, I double back up the street and then over a block. I then go back down this street and approach the target from the side. Slowly, I sneak up on my prey like a trained predator, keeping to the shadows. I get to the edge of the street that separates the block I'm on and my target. Grabbing the knife by the blade, I pull it out from my pocket, palm it blade down, and tuck it into my sleeve.

I then head across the road like I was taking a stroll. The thug realizes I'm approaching when I'm about all the way across. I fling my knife straight out as he appears from the shadows. It flies through the air before impaling itself into the neck of the scoundrel. Blood gurgles from his mouth, and as I near him, I see the panic in his eyes. I watch his chest rise and fall for the last time, and when I see his eyes staring into nothingness, I remove my blade, fighting a wet suction. As I rise, I approach the door he was guarding, wondering if it was locked, but when I place my hand on it, it swings open easily.

Try before you pry, I remember an old fire chief once saying.

I slip into the building like a ghost, swapping my weapons and checking that I have one in the chamber; I know I do, but it's a good habit. Letting the door glide back and bump into my heel before I silently close it behind, I twist the silencer into place. I raise my weapon, confident and assured that only three people will leave this place alive tonight. This has gone too far, and now my friends are involved.

You invited the devil to the dance; now it's time to party.

Clearing my mind of all emotions and centering myself, I close my eyes briefly, pushing humanity and empathy to the side. Then, stashing it away in the box of my mind, the lid closes with a cold certainty. I move off at a calculated pace, carefully hunting for the perpetrators; from what I could hear as I was listening in, there are only three. I'm moving stealthily down a dark hallway and approaching an open doorway. Light spills out from it as I creep closer and closer. I peek around the corner, then hide again. It looks like a large loading dock area, and I don't see anyone around. After a brief second look, I can see the place is completely empty, or so it seems to be. I visualize my friends needing me, and panic rises. I have to shut off that emotion. It'll make me sloppy. I cross the doorway and continue, stopping at the hallway's corner, then sliding around it. I see a thug with a nasty scar holding a cup of ramen, and I give him two bullets to chew on. Strolling over to his open-mouthed corpse, I notice the noodles dangling down from his lips and onto the floor.

I kick the Styrofoam cup to the side as I pass. Moving further along, the space opens up to a large room. It's a breakroom, based on the mismatched couches, a pack of water bottles on the table, and other second-hand stuff. Nothing but the best for my boys, the foreman probably thought. I cross quickly to the other side and look out a dirty window into a maintenance area beyond. The area is dark, and I see light spilling from a side room. I move to the room's other exit and slip silently forward, hunting. I approach the open doorway from a distance, scanning inside while remaining invisible to anyone in there. I see a tough guy with a leather wrist strap walking around, kicking the chair of a woman tied up, taunting her.

Aria!

I approach the room rapidly, firing on the move. I hit him twice above center mass and he spins, falling into a hyperventilating Aria. I kick him off her squirming form and scan the room. No one else is here, and I snatch the hood from her head. She blinks, looking up into my face through tear-stained eyes. I look around, find a box cutter, and start in on her bindings. I set my gun on the ground next to the chair. As I saw through the ropes, I glanced over the room.

"I'll get you out as quickly as I can. Are you hurt?"

"I'm super freaked out, and my head is throbbing. I need some water, please."

I quickly head back into the janky breakroom and grab two water bottles. On my way back, I listen intently for noise or anyone in my immediate area. Not hearing anything, I enter the room again and hold the bottle to her dry, cracked lips. She guzzles the water as I tilt the bottle up. She gasps thanks as I go back to sawing through her binds. With a jerk, I cut the last resistance away, and the rope loosens as I unwrap it from around her. She slumps forward, and I briefly steady her as she recollects herself.

"I heard Avery fighting, and I think they hurt her badly."

I scan the room and floor, my eyes stopping in a large pool of blood. There are drag marks, and I follow them out the door. I trace the trail of blood drops, likely from her being over someone's shoulder. They go around another corner and through a closed meat locker. The power is on, and the latch has a time lock. Looking back at Aria, I can see she can't help. She's still collecting herself, but I don't think the lock could be hacked, even if she was top-notch. I move around the immediate area, stressing a little, looking around for something to help get me through the door or past the lock. I rush back into the main garage, looking for options through the shelves and storage spots.

I need to build a bomb.

Chapter Fourteen

I gather my supplies in an old egg crate and return to the door. I need to shape the charge and work to reinforce the backing to make sure it directs most of the force forward. I place a large, thick piece of metal sheeting over the mix of chemicals and secure a bag of powdery oxidizer inside. I then run wires, stripped from the wall, into the bag, grabbing a car battery and the other end of the wires, as we duck around the corner.

I look at Aria beside me behind the wall and touch the positive end of the battery with the wire. The effect is instantaneous and violent. The explosion sends the metal sheet flying back to hit the wall, crumpling the metal. The explosion sheared through the lock and has partially blown the door in.

Our ears popped from the overpressure, and I shake my head to clear the effects, already moving around the corner and into the smoking breach. As I push through the opening, I kick the door in more and am hit by the cold wave of freezer air. My mind goes to fire and snow, and I plead silently for my tortured psyche to take a break. I vigorously shake my head, unaware of the tears in my eyes.

Not now, please!

"Avery!"

I search inside. The explosion has destroyed the light switch, and I search deeper and deeper into the cold, dark tomb. The only light is from the ruined doorway, and my eyes dart around, searching. I see the tip of her shoe and rush over to her. She's unconscious, and I search for a pulse.

Please!

A soft beat brushes my fingertip, and I exhale a breath I didn't even know I was holding. I scoop her into my arms and walk back when I see Aria pulling the door away. She partly succeeds, and I turn sideways to squeeze through the gap, unwilling to stop and put Avery down.

"She's alive, but hurt badly. She has a shallow pulse, but we need to control this bleeding before we move her."

The cold had slowed the bleeding, but as she warms up, the blood flows faster out of her ravaged face.

This is all my fault.

Aria sees the look on my face.

"Hurry up and bring her over here..."

"...and don't even think about it. This is not your fault. These bastards did this. Look at her poor face!"

I gently lay her down and stand, backing away as Aria helps her twin, identical no more. Tears are running down her cheek as she works to bind her sister's gaping flesh back against her skull. She's expertly wrapping parts, but I know we need to go. Before I leave the room, I turn and see Tiny entering the room, wondering what that noise was.

Holy crap, this guy is enormous!

"Hey, bro!"

I say this casually, like I don't have a care. He looks confused for a second, and I reach behind my back to discover I never picked up my gun.

What a rookie mistake.

I see his face contort from stupid wonder to angry toddler, and I know I'm in trouble. I move away from the Storm sisters, Aria barely looking up as she continues caring for her sister. Luckily, his eyes and stupid feet follow me, and I need to think fast.

I back out of the little room through the other exit, and I find myself back in the maintenance area. I'm frantically looking for a weapon when Tiny catches up to me. He swings at my head, and I duck under his fist just in time. I feel the wind from his passing arm on the back of my neck as I maneuver my body underneath the blow. I turn and deliver an uppercut, giving it all I have, but it barely moves his head.

Uh oh.

He's strong, but I'm faster, so the game changes quickly. I deliver a series of rabbit punches to his kidneys, jumping back and dodging his clumsy attempts to strike me. He has always relied on his size and general pleasant attitude to get to this point, which may have worked with others, but he has "*Never Had a Friend Like Me!*"

RIP Tupac.

I continue to move around him, and he gets frustrated. As each second passes, he gets a bit more furious. I'm a little cocky, and I taunt him, missing his next telegraphed move. He connects a left to my right eye socket, and I swear I see the future for a second. I shake my head, still moving sideways from the hit, and he gets me again smack dab in the ribs.

I think he cracked one.

I fight to catch my breath as I back away, and he strides toward me like a victorious shitbird, and I hate him even more, if that is possible. I didn't want to flip this switch, but my plans changed, and if I wanted to survive the next few minutes, I had better react using all my skills accordingly.

This fat piece of shit doesn't know what is about to happen. He fucked up.

I'm bleeding from my eyebrow, and my lips skew into a sadistic grin as I look up. Lowering my head subtly, I stare at him with eyes as hard as a virgin's dick on prom night. Blood drips to the dirty cement floor, and he thinks it's an act and continues, as my smile grows slightly bigger.

Practice.

When the switch is flipped, I feel like I slide back into my body, and a terrifying demon from hell itself takes over. At this point, I don't have a line anymore...at all.

When he's close enough, I launch myself toward him, and my strong fingers gouge into both of his eyes, hard with retribution. He backs up a step, panic seeping into his shocked yet massive body, and as his eyes redden and bulge out, they pool blood down his fat cheeks. I then jump forward, and with the palms of my hands, I slap the sides of his head, rupturing his eardrums with a clap. He screams like a little bitch as he loses both his shit and his equilibrium. Sinking to his knees, he fights gravity, and taking advantage of his position, I slice his throat with the sharp-edged blade of the knife that has been a part of me for so many years. The carry-through rips apart his windpipe, and he makes a sharp whistling sound. Startled, his hand shakes, then goes up to his neck involuntarily. With a roundhouse kick to the side of his head, I finish his miserable life once and for all by detaching that blob of a dome from his body and knocking it across the room. The momentum from the kick sends his headless body down to the ground for the last time, like a giant, ugly, bug-infested tree.

Coming back from a terrifying place, I shake off the severity of the situation and take a moment to collect myself. I return to the room I found Aria in, shaking my head. I collect my gun, which is surprisingly still sitting by her chair. I creep back into the hallway, checking to see whether there are any more surprises.

I'll make it quick, but that last victory was more luck than any-thing.

When I hear an engine close by, I immediately clear the building and return through the dark corridor. I'm about to cross the threshold when I hear the building's roll-up garage door rattle, rise, and then jerk. I put my back to the wall and listen intently to the sound of an engine driving into the space and its brakes squealing. The motor turns off with a sputter, and I hear the doors open. The sound of shoes walking on gritty cement gently echoes around the space as the car doors slam shut.

Now what?

Milling around momentarily, they talk amongst themselves in a hushed but hurried manner. I count the unfriendly individuals and hear slides click as weapon magazines are seated. I immediately eject my magazine, effectively counting the rounds.

Eight.

As I slide in the magazine, I feel the satisfying click as it locks back into place. I have extra magazines pressed against my side, making me feel safe and assured, knowing that I have more rounds right here on my body. But the thing is, in a gunfight, split seconds are crucial, and any sway of attention is almost always deadly. I don't want to get stuck in this. Avery is badly hurt, and every second is critical. My already elevated stress ratchets up another notch, and my stomach tightens.

I will save my friend, full stop!

I'm about to enter from the doorway, guns blazing, when a startled thug walks right into me as I exit. I have my weapon in a ready position, lowered as I was turning. I bring it up, planting two precious rounds into this poor slob, soon to be a pile of cold flesh. He's going down but not fast enough, so I boot his chest, sending him flying forward as I aim at my next target.

I surprise myself sometimes; this time, let's just say it was good.

I certainly have enough momentum after I boot the guy, so I fall to my knees, carrying the fall and then slid forward, scooping up his gun.

My government training kicks in with a vengeance, and carrying a weapon in each hand, I rise heroically like the mighty war demon I am. I worked hard for this accomplishment; no dirtbag will steal my thunder, nor my life. Sparks flash as bullets hit the surrounding area, and shells fall nearby, clinking with a sharp, tinny landing. I took these wanna-be gangsters by surprise, but my advantage will only last for so long. I strike out another goon by the car, a tough-looking woman with a full-sleeve tattoo of fire and a creepy devil done up Japanese-style. When my rounds strike her stocky frame, she has a look of confusion that slowly turns to anguished panic as she registers her life nearing its end.

Moving through the gunfire and smoke, I make my way up to the side of the vehicle right next to where she collapsed, staying low and dodging the aimed shots. As the impacting bullets hit the front windshield and the hood of the car, our eyes lock for a second.

Her tough facade and demeanor melt away as she realizes her clock is about to stop ticking. She probably wondered at some point in her life about how she would die, and I bet my bottom dollar she never thought it would be from bleeding out on the cold, dirty cement floor of a meat factory and right next to a stranger. All for nothing. Although money was probably her motivator, you can't spend that money when you're six feet under. I watch her eyes lose focus. Her pupils dilate as her soul leaves her body for parts unknown.

I shake my head at that waste of a human being and return to the fight. I hear someone trying to flank me from the side, and I quickly move that way to intercept them. The difference between a savvy, street-trained tough guy and a worldly professional government-trained killer simply comes down to two things: speed and violence.

Applying these principles as he approaches, I meet the apprehensive hitman and smash him in the mouth with the butt of my pistol, shattering all his teeth. We are standing right next to each other as I grab his thick neck, violently wrenching it to the right. I hear a wet charck, and he falls like a sack of rotten potatoes.

Stalking like a panther, I move past his bloody lump of a corpse and attempt to control my anger. I want to kill all these motherfuckers, but I need to catch one alive so I can torture the fuck out of someone to leak intel. Another goon fires at me, and I send one spiraling into his left eye. He drops, and I cross off another potential problem from my list of things to do. I hear someone screaming orders in a shrill voice, clearly in a state of panic. The woman sounds like a frightened bird squawking at her rapidly diminishing muscle force. Someone says her name, Texas. I realize she's who I want, obviously the group's mouthpiece. There is only one more guy, and I try not to get cocky. The end of the battle is always the most important part; you need to finish it decisively and definitively.

I appreciate and pay special attention to all the double D's.

Working slowly toward the shrill overlord, I'm blindsided by her last cohort. He's a fat, sloppy son of a bitch, and he propels my body with great force, ramming me straight into a concrete wall. We grapple for my weapon, and I notice his gun is still in its holster on his hip. I headbutt him, then eject my magazine, and pull the trigger, clearing the weapon before letting go. Through watery eyes, he victoriously leaps back, rotating my gun to fire at me, but the last thing he sees after hearing an empty click, is me pulling the trigger of his weapon and delivering three of his bullets straight into the empty void of his brainpan.

Nighty night asshole.

I pick up my weapon and insert a fresh magazine from my belt. I crouch down and pick up my old mag, putting it in my pocket as I hunt for the leader. She has gone quiet, but I can still hear her chirpy, panicked breathing as I get closer. Hearing a slight whistling noise that sounds like a multi-orgasmic teapot, I slide around the corner, my weapon trained directly on the bird woman. She scoots backward, startled, and the flute ceases momentarily before spiking. Approaching her in a casual yet smooth demeanor, it's my eyes that speak loudly and announce to her she's fucked.

Howya doing, Tex-ass?

As she looks toward me, I can tell she's scared shitless, but I'm struck and momentarily taken aback by her uncanny resemblance to Toucan Sam from the Froot Loops cereal box. Her nose is enormous, and her face sweats beads of panic. She wears an elaborate, frumpy cowboy outfit that makes her look like a rodeo clown. Hideously insane looking, she's wearing fake rhinestones bedazzled across and up and down her jacket and pants. She wears thick orthopedic shoes, and I notice she's missing a thumb as she covers her face with her hands. She looks like she pecks when she talks.

"Don't hurt me. I will get you whatever you want."

Wearing a Cheshire cat grin, I close in on her, and as my shadow falls across her horrified face, I watch her eyes grow to the size of saucers.

"I want you."

Chapter Fifteen

I muscle Texas into the trunk of her own Cadillac, thinking what a generic nickname. How many bland, non-imaginative people gave themselves the same moniker? That's just mean to Texas. As I slam the trunk on her panic-stricken face, I can't help but be opinionated.

"Texas? That's a stupid name."

I hear Aria call my name, so I rush across the room to the other side and find her staring at me, startled and blank-faced.

"I got us a ride. Let's move."

Running back to Avery, I scoop her up from the floor. The heavier-than-usual weight tells me she's still unconscious. I run back to the car, carrying the injured Storm sister, and I hear Aria gasp when she sees all the blood and guts in the central area of the meat warehouse. It's like a scene in a horror movie, but this time it's real. A decapitated head tilts creepily against a stack of wooden pallets. The eyes are gouged, lopsided, and grotesque. The bloody footprints crisscross the area. Shiny shell casings litter the floor, and there is still a thin layer of gun smoke lingering in the air. It might look different, but the end of a fight always smells the same.

Gunpowder and blood.

I gently lower Avery into the vehicle's back seat and then rush over to release the chain latch on the roll-up doors.

Aria dashes over to join her sister, who is fading away. As soon as there is enough clearance for the car to exit, I floor the gas pedal and attempt to speed off into the night. The Cadillac handles like a giant boat, and it's nearly impossible to drive fast. Finally, when I catch on to its weird operating system, I push the beast to its limit. I maneuver the vessel down the street like a pro, accelerating on the straightaways and slamming on the brakes before whipping around the corners. I continue to push this car to its maximum, and I will be surprised if there is any rubber left on the tires by the time we get to the hospital.

Looking through the rearview mirror, I check on Aria and notice her crying silently. I can't imagine the pain and agony she's experiencing at this moment. If we weren't in such a hurry, I would brake-check Texas just to bang her up and possibly slam her beak into the side of the trunk.

The light from early dawn appears, coloring the clouds, and I know it will be a long day. I see the hospital up ahead and whisper a sincere please and a grateful thank you to the guy upstairs.

With all tires screeching to a halt, we slide into the emergency department drop-off area, and I'm out the door before the car has even stopped. With a rent-a-cop chasing after me, screaming obscenities for parking in the red, I'm yelling for help - my every word falling upon deaf ears. I run to the rear door, and the rent-a-cop grabs my shirt, attempting to stop me. I fling open the door, Aria helping me get a hold of her stricken twin. I'm racing to the emergency room carrying Avery, her arm dangling loosely at her side, the security guard hot on my tail. I flag down a passing doctor. When he notices the amount of blood, he allows us to enter the triage center, sending the pissed-off guard back to his post. He then calls someone to expedite her admission. I don't want to put her down or waste time; everyone is moving quickly. A doctor calls out from the open double doors, motioning for me to come his way. I follow him into an unoccupied examination room. Worried nurses and doctors scramble behind me, already calling out orders and demands for supplies. I set Avery on the bed and then back away as the hospital staff swallow her up. They work quickly, without panic, as they attempt to save Avery's life. I shuffle away from the commotion, numb, not even realizing that my shirt is soaked with my friend's blood.

After a kind old nurse gives me a scrub top and I change, I return to the front desk and fill out the hospital paper-work. I use a health insurance policy in situations such as this, and thankfully, I have memorized the policy number. That is another little benefit the U.S. Gov. thought to give me. Even a spy needs a checkup occasionally. I tell Aria I will be back, then return to the car. Aria checks in with the nurse at the front desk and then goes to sit in the waiting area. I wish I could be there for my friend, but I have other things to take care of. As I head back to the car, my blood begins to boil.

Texas and I are going to have a little talk, and I know the perfect place to take that bird.

I hop in and accelerate, then slam on the brakes multiple times as I leave the parking lot. Whenever I approached a speed bump, I would floor it and ride this bucking bronco like a rodeo king. I hear her body banging around the trunk and hitting the lid.

I exit the facility lot, wishing there had been more bumps and dips.

I head to a spot I know, a graffiti-stained runoff drain leading into the giant aqueduct system crisscrossing this crazy city like scars.

We arrive about fifteen minutes later, and I haven't cooled down at all. I'm still furious as I storm out of the Caddy. Upon flinging open the back lid, I'm assaulted by the smell of piss. Texas blinks away tears as the sun's brightness blinds her. I forcefully pull her from the depths of the trunk and dump her frumpy, pear-shaped body hard onto the cement. Her panicked eyes search for help, and she shakes violently when she realizes it's just the two of us. Standing over her, I laugh as she scoots away, sliding uncomfortably across the gravely concrete.

I would never deliberately hurt an innocent woman, but I'm struggling with this one here.

But is she innocent? I think not.

My mother raised me right, but I would bet my life that she would even want to slap this horrible person as hard as she could. I do want to hit her, but I can't quite bring myself to that place. I pace back and forth, figuring out my next move. Texas watches me with enormous eyes, bright enough to keep her big beak shut.

"Who are you, lady? Don't lie. You're going to give me all the information I ask for!"

Danger drips off each word I speak, and I can read her pretty well. She's terrified. I can quickly get my answers if I keep the pressure up.

"Please don't hurt me. I'll cooperate. I'm Birdy, Birdy Flat-bore-Fowler...who are you?"

She flinches again, her thumbless hand covering her face as I lean into her perception of me. She sounds like she's almost in awe, and I secretly grin as I high-five my demon.

That's right!

"Shut up! I'm the one asking the questions. What the fuck are you up to? Why'd you try to kill me? I don't even know who you are! I mean, seriously, who the fuck are you?"

I watch her as I back up, and I can tell Birdy realizes I won't hurt her. I see her demeanor change, and she smiles.

"Oh, you are one of those guys, huh? A gentleman?"

She stands and puts her hands on her oversized hips.

"Too nice for your own..."

I cut her off, as the back of my hand catches her across the mouth. She wobbles and then falls backward onto the ground in shock. I whip out my pistol from behind my back and fire two rounds, which hit the cement, closely to either side of her odd-shaped head. A piece of concrete that chipped off with the bullet's impact sliced a small line across her cheek. Blood weeps out, and her eyes are back to the big panicking moons.

This chick is dumb as fuck.

"Lady, I was giving you a chance, but now, not so much."

I walk up to her like an avenging angel, and with my smoking weapon rising toward her paling face, she pisses her pants once again.

"Uh...uh... the locker, that crypto thing... you know? Oleg worked for my aunt, who made a fortune in black-market smuggling. He was her accountant for years but planned to take all the money and disappear as their partnership soured."

She puts her hands up to block her face, and I can't help but laugh at her.

"Continue."

"Okay...okay... Oleg transferred the money from all the accounts, crypto wallets, and everything else. He merged them into that locker. Whoever has the locker has access to all the money. But there is a code you need to enter to get to it. Before Aunt Harriet died, she was having some heavy mental problems and left all the money to her little dog, Bunny."

"Hold on. Are you telling me that the money belongs to a dog?"

"Yes...and from what I have been told, my aunt gave no one the code. Well, except for Bunny, of course."

"Except for Bunny, huh? Alright then, tell me more about this Bunny money."

My internal child cracks up as I mean mug the squawking bird from Texas.

"I...I... um... um... I heard this from Jenny, my cousin. She asked for my help because she told me she was doing something else. Another job, but she wouldn't say what it was. I came to help run a crew for her. Jenny is the one who knows how this all fits together. Please...please... don't hurt me. I'm telling you the truth. I...I... swear."

I can tell she's not lying, and my mind is racing, trying to put this puzzle together.

What did I get thrust into this time?

I didn't want any of this drama, and if I ever see Jahvey again, I'm going to kill him.

"You said your cousin is doing something else. What?"

Texas squirms under my contemptuous gaze, and I shake my head deliberately.

"I swear...all she told me was that It's some kind of revenge. That is all she said. Jenny likes to keep things separate, compartmentalized, as she calls it. I don't know!"

She shrieks out this last part in an ear-splitting whine.

Who's torturing who here?

Backing up, I motion for her to stand and shut her mouth. She reluctantly does so, and I back up another pace, more out of habit than of need. She's shaking in her orthopedic slipper-boots, and a few rhinestones fall off, embellishing the asphalt with glistening colors.

What's up with those, anyway? On second thought, I don't want to know!

My phone buzzes, and I glance at the screen. It's a message from Mrs. James.

I glance over at Texas and notice her peering at my phone. Her demeanor has changed, and I don't know if she still takes all this as a threat. Looking down again, I read the entire text. Mrs. James says that she will drop off Alley in an hour. I need to wrap this up. I have to stop at the hospital and check on my friends. I'm being pulled in several directions and beginning to feel the strain. Looking back at Texas, I know she can read my thoughts as soon as I think them.

I cock my head to the side, and a smile slides onto my face like an evil promise. Texas sees this and involuntary shudders, and I can't help but suppress a laugh at the sheer lunacy I see before me. I want to send her an obvious message, but I'm done with killing unless it's called for.

As I stroll toward the terrified rhinestone cowbird, she backs up, whistling worried little ess' until she gets to the embankment's edge.

"Listen, Sparkles, killing you would be more trouble than you're worth. If we ever meet again, your value will skyrocket. Are we clear?"

She stands at attention, nodding emphatically and shaking in fear. Instantly, I'm blinded by her rhinestones and sequins, which catch the sun's rays, making the area around her look like a disco.

"Get the fuck out of here! Now! If you're smart, which I doubt, you'll buy yourself a one-way ticket and leave the country immediately."

She hurtles past me, bursting into tears. For about half a second, I felt sorry for the old bird, but when I remember what they did to Avery, all I feel is the need for revenge.

I wonder if I made the right decision.

Once the unpleasantness of that situation is over, I drive the Caddy up to the top of the access way and park. I sit for a moment in silence, then call for a ride. As I wait in the car, I wrestle with the information I had just learned.

Oleg was the accountant of Harriet Fowler, a name I had heard before. But as she slipped further and further into dementia, Oleg's plan to embezzle her money went into action. He merged all the distinct accounts into that crypto-locker, and whoever has the code, other than Bunny, has access to the digital money.

Whatever happened to good old cash? The world is such a different place.

Pondering that somber thought, my ride pulls up. I walk out of the tunnel, leaving the memories of that four-wheeled boat behind in the dust. I'll never forget being the last passenger in that humongous vehicle. Walking away from the flames of the fire I had just lit on the seat of that charter, I watch it grow into a blaze of glory. When I enter my driver's car and set off on our way, the raging inferno breaks out and mixes with the highly flammable gasoline fumes from the car's tank. As the guy speeds off, we hear a loud blast of a boom from behind. The semi-concerned driver looks into his side-view mirror for about a millisecond before returning to the audiobook he was listening to.

I hope it's a good book.

Chapter Sixteen

And now, for a fever dream...

Texas...Birdy Fowler...everything about this woman was just not right...except for her name. Her parents certainly chose an appropriate label for this misfit. Growing up, Birdy was bullied, and it probably had something to do with her speech impairment and her odd-shaped nose, which together made her whistle whenever she spoke.

Her parents and other family members rejected her, and they all washed their hands of her the moment she turned eighteen. The only person in her family who would have anything to do with her was her cousin, Jenny.

Birdy left her hometown of Pickaweed, Alabama, and began her journey to Masserro, California - mode of transportation - a huge four-door Oldsmobile. Jenny lived in Masserro and so did their Aunt Harriet, and Birdy planned to surprise them both. She quickly crossed county and state lines, never stopping too long at any one point. That is until her car broke down right in the middle of nowhere. Frustrated, she looked in every direction, and all she could see were vultures and tumbleweed. Abandoning her car, she began walking, promising herself that she would buy some comfortable shoes or slippers as soon as she reached civilization.

Birdy plodded down the unpaved road, dodging balls of Russian thistle for hours and hours, then out of nowhere, appeared a sign. She was smack dab in the middle of Effluvium, Texas - population sixty-eight. Mad, exhausted, very thirsty, and although difficult, she continued on until she saw a house in the near distance. Trudging away, she headed straight toward the only option available.

Friend or foe...did it really matter?

When she was about to set foot on the property, she stopped for a quick second from the edge of the dirt road. She realized that what she had been hiking toward was an empty farm. Birdy walked down a pathway that looked like *"Beer Can Alley"* and the closer she got to the old, dilapidated house with broken windows, the more she believed it was deserted as well. She climbed the few steps to the front porch and almost fell through a plank of rotten wood. When she let out a high-pitched squeal of a whistle, a gigantic hairy man opened the front door and grabbed Birdy's wing...I mean arm. He yanked her inside, closed the front door, and then hauled her squawking ass down to the basement. He shackled her ankles and kept her hidden downstairs in the dark for seven years.

Roger Flatbore was the name of the man that had taken poor Birdy hostage, and although unbelievable, her whistling screeches that escaped from under the locked door seduced him. It calmed and comforted him. You know, it took the edge off, even during those really tough times.

Roger and Birdy would often compete in a romantic game of thumb wrestling, but it wasn't long before Roger got tired of losing to his hook-nosed seductress. He had a competitive nature and when he lost, he would go into his closet and cry for an hour.

Although Roger lost many a game, he still had a special surprise planned for the seventh anniversary of her kidnapping.

When that special day arrived, Roger took delight in amputating Birdy's thumb. He coated it in chocolate and then rolled it in nuts and stored it in the freezer. It was a ceremonial occasion, a special event, and a most glorious day, one he will always remember.

So will Birdy.

After all the excitement and when Birdy finished bandaging her bloody stub, Roger demanded a tune, but not until Birdy washed the bloody knife and all the dirty dishes. When she was done, she strolled over to the corner by the fireplace, stood on a wooden chair, and began speaking. Roger sat down on the old, tattered couch and became excited, very aroused. He began squeezing his thighs together rapidly, attempting to extinguish the fire below. Having little to no restraint, he finally broke down and unzipped his hefty-sized pants and stroked his wand to the cadence of Birdy's voice.

After the satisfying musical, Roger allowed Birdy to stay outside for a couple extra hours, alongside him, of course. He had gotten used to her company, but it was the perfect pitch of her whistle that really turned him on. It got to the point when he kept her locked in the basement for only fifteen hours a day. Roger had decided that he was going to propose to Birdy soon, but there was a catch.

Isn't there always?

You see, Roger was a crafty guy, and he made a human-sized bird perch for Birdy. He gathered logs and feathers from the property and carved away. It took him a long time, but when the final coat of glue dried, her perch was ready. He even tied a big red bow on it.

He went to the basement and unlocked the shackles from around Birdy's thick ankles and grabbed her thumbless hand. He guided her upstairs and presented her with the handmade gift. She glanced at the perch, at him, then at the chair, and finally her happy eyes jetted straight back to the perch. Smiling so big her nose touched her mouth, she looked at Roger endearingly. Birdy had never received a gift from anyone before, not even her parents or family, and she was at a loss for words...bad timing.

Roger ordered her to hop up on the perch right then and there and whistle a shrill ditty of gratitude. Then, after a blissful hour of extreme thigh friction, he declared she must perform for him three or four times a day, each show lasting at least an hour. Birdy really loved her time on the perch, and it showed in her expression.

Is that a tear?

Roger was delighted with the melodic chime-like yodeling and was falling more and more in love with Birdy. He knew that if he wanted to live harmoniously, he would have to make her his wife. So, using his crafty skills, Roger made an engagement ring for his thumbless little songbird.

He went to unlock the safe and pulled out his special box, the finest collection of rhinestones ever. Sorting through the individual fake gems, he finally found the perfect one. He admired the artificial stone and then contemplated using sequins instead. But his pick of the lot and its sparkling attributes helped Roger decide.

He glued the shiny piece of plastic to a small-sized key ring and held on to it for quite some time. He wasn't ready to give up his bachelor status, even though he had never been in a relationship or even gone out on a date.

Finally, when Roger decided it was time, he became so nervous that he broke out in a terrible case of hives which covered every inch of his body. For three whole days, Birdy begged and pleaded to come out of the basement, but Roger refused. When the rash finally cleared, he released her, and the first thing she did was complain about being thirsty.

Because of dehydration, when she spoke, she no longer whistled. Roger panicked as he rushed to the sink in a frenzy and filled a huge jug with water, then forced Birdy to drink the entire thing. He needed those blaring flute-shrieks to come back right away, and fortunately for him, they did. And to his delight, they were louder and more shrill. They sounded just like the toots from a steam-rolled bagpipe.

As soon as the first whistle slipped from Birdy's mouth, she was right back up on the perch again, and Roger unzipped his pants and was right back on the couch.

Eventually, the two got married by the town's mascot, but that didn't happen until Birdy's musical tone and vocals were back to perfect pitch.

Birdy spent her married years basically in the same manner as she had before. The only thing that differed was that now, at night, Roger would come down to the basement and shackle himself to Birdy for some relief. He needed to hear that final whistle of the day before he went back upstairs to go to sleep.

Yes, her husband was a peculiar man, but he was a man of many talents. He loved to knit ponchos and oversized capes. And on the rare occasion when he brought out his sewing machine, he made drawstring bags and cloth shoes. But what he loved the most was collecting counterfeit rhinestones and sequins, and with Birdy's fondness for things that sparkle. She adorned the entire house, furniture included, with a variety of bedazzled accents.

Her fascination for flashy frocks had begun.

Everything was fantastic, just wonderful, and the couple enjoyed married bliss for another twelve years or so. Roger loved his Birdy, and he experienced a satisfying relaxation each time she hopped onto her perch and whistled.

He had demanded more of her time, and she was a willing participant. Once the shackles were off, she was eager, but her atrophied muscles couldn't make it up the stairs without resting halfway. She was in excruciating pain. Birdy didn't care much for the shackles because they were too tight on her thick cankles. Plus, with her edema, they left marks and terrible indentations.

Many great things came from this relationship, but the most apparent was that Roger had become a musically satisfied and much more glamourous man. One day, while the two lovebirds were eating dinner, a huge rhinestone popped off a lampshade and flew through the air. It landed in Roger's mouth, got stuck in his windpipe, and right in front of his

panicking pigeon, he choked to death on a piece of his favorite hobby.

Birdy refused to let the razzle-dazzle die with him, so she had
the mortician pluck out his eyes and put huge rhinestones in
the sockets. The service was brilliant, to say the least, with
Birdy whistling and squawking out Roger's favorite tunes.
Birdy left Effluvium after burying Roger. She hopped into
his bubblegum-pink wing-tipped Cadillac and continued her
long overdue trip to Masserro. She was a lot older now and
believed that she had all the answers to life's questions.

Not bad for someone locked in a basement for almost twenty
years.

Birdy was in shock when she saw how much the world
had changed during her twenty-year absence while driving
across the country.

Once in Masserro, she went straight to her Aunt Harriet's
house. The welcome she got wasn't as warm as expected, and she never imagined that her aunt would be gone.
Regardless, when Jenny answered the door, Birdy almost
immediately asked if she could stay in the guest room for a
few weeks or a month. Jenny, who was still grieving the death
of her husband and of course her aunt, told Birdy she could
stay for a while. She then mentioned a bit about what had
happened with their Aunt Harriet, you know, the dementia,
her death and, of course, Bunny, the billionaire dog.

But she didn't tell her everything...

Jenny used to take advantage of Birdy's ignorance and
planned to continue to do so. There was a lot going on, and
she knew she would need help with something. As long as
Birdy didn't know too many of the details, everything would
be fine.

Jenny and Birdy had lived together before. After Jenny's parents were killed in a terrible blimp accident, she moved in
with Birdy and Birdy's parents. The two girls were about the
same age, around sixteen or seventeen, but neither one re-

ally had any type of supervision or discipline. Birdy's parents ignored them both like they were invisible, and they would not let either girl speak.

Probably thought Jenny whistled, too.

Regardless, they were an odd family, and things didn't change when Jenny moved in. Birdy and Jenny both left when they turned eighteen, with Jenny leaving first and Birdy leaving about six months later. They had planned to meet up in Masserro, but Birdy's pit-stop in Effluvium lasted longer than she could have ever imagined. They had both grown up, albeit in entirely different ways, but now they were back together this time as adults.

Jenny got married when she was about twenty and she had a wonderful husband who was in the military. He provided her with love and affection. Jenny was a fantastic cook and the perfect housewife. Although she was unable to have children, her husband made up for that emptiness. She couldn't have asked for more, except for him to still be alive. She had already suffered through the death of her parents, then, after about thirteen years of marriage, her husband passed, leaving Jenny a grieving widow. Jenny swore to herself that she would never get involved with anyone who had the potential to break her heart.

When she first moved to Masserro, she met many people, mostly guys, who took her to clubs, restaurants and bars. Jenny was a party girl, but when she met her husband, she immediately changed. Knowing the worth of what they had, she poured out all her love for him. Jenny was as loyal as they come.

Jenny would often spend time with her Aunt Harriet, both personally and for business. The darker side intrigued her, and she wanted to explore it fully. Her aunt taught Jenny how things worked in the underground operation, and she learned things quickly.

Harriet Fowler's mental health was deteriorating at a rapid pace, and she paid a corrupt lawyer a large sum of money to change her will, making her dog Bunny the sole beneficiary. Jenny was furious when she found out. She discovered a lot more than that had been secretly happening in the business, and after her aunt's death, she was denied entry and access to everything. The will only mentioned her name once, appointing her as the caretaker of the mansion and Bunny. Both loss and rage overtook Jenny. Her husband was gone, and so was her inheritance. Revenge was the only thing on her mind. She wanted her piece of the pie, and swore that one way or another, she would get it.

But would she be able to eat it?

Chapter Seventeen

Contacted through Harriet Fowler's dark network, Jiro Kawakami was one of the last real ninjas in the world. Sadly, he will be the last member of his family in the Ban clan. The world had moved on, and he was discovering this new digital one with its unique skills. He felt like a man standing over a chasm with the old on one side and the new on the other. He liked to create metaphorical images and movies to reinforce his concepts, as he was internalizing his deep thoughts.

They contacted him because he was nearby and possessed the particular skill set needed for this clean-up mission. It was early morning when he arrived at the meat processing plant, and this was time sensitive. He would make double the money for this.

Easy money!

He silently entered through an unlocked door, adjusted his backpack, and formulated a plan. He needed to make the physical evidence go away—the bodies, blood, weapons, brass casings from the gun battles, any hard evidence, every-thing.

And the sun was currently rising on another workday.

He had 30 minutes, if he was lucky, before people started showing up for work. He discovered this when he found their timecards and punch clock as he did a quick walk-through. As he was doing this, he was collecting any weapon he found and putting them in a canvas bag he had. He unrolled. He found the digital storage for the security cameras in the manager's office and collected the physical drive. He then went into the main maintenance area where he had seen a forklift and unhooked the propane. He returned to the main area with the bodies and placed the propane tank on the ground beside a corpse with a startled look on his face.

Jiro pulled a large plastic container filled with a special powder out of his backpack and sifted it onto the floor and surfaces as he made his way through the facility. He sprinkled liberal amounts around the bodies and then replaced one of the lamp lights with a special lightbulb he pulled out of a padded pocket in his backpack. He had drilled a hole and filled the inside with gunpowder up far enough to bury the filament before sealing it with superglue.

He peeks outside and then exits when he sees no one is around yet, with his bag of guns. He hides this across the street and then returns, slipping back inside. He looks around, scanning for anything he might have missed, then turns on the propane and attaches a few balloons with ammonia powder. When the propane explodes, this will aerosolize into the air, creating a strong odor. This mixed with the powder he sprinkled, which acts explosively when it gets wet, should give the impression that this was a meth lab explosion.

When you can't make it disappear, you can redirect the view.

When he's sure everything is in place, and intelligence-wise it's as sterile as he has time for, he heads for the door, with five minutes remaining by his estimate before anyone will be here. As he's leaving, he flips the light switch and exits the facility as explosions start to go off in the maintenance area behind him.

The fire triggers the sprinkler system and the whole place erupts in a violent, super-heated fire that begins to consume all the evidence, burning so hot as to even melt the brass. The heat coming off the blaze is brutal, and Jiro feels it pulsing into his back as he walks across the street. The air reeks of strong ammonia and the fire burns with vivid shades of purple and blue. He nods to himself on a job well done, collects his sack of guns, and heads towards his car as he hears sirens approaching from the distance.

Chapter Eighteen

I'm home, waiting outside with a big cheesy smile, when Mrs. James silently glides toward me, pulling up to the curb in a small electric vehicle. When I see a coned Alley sitting shotgun with her head hanging out of the window and her tongue flapping wildly, I instantly forget about Texas. I notice her tail is wagging so quickly, and the excitement I see in her tells me she's happy to see me too.

I'm talking about Alley, not Mrs. James.

Mrs. James pulls to the curb, parks, and exits the vehicle. She walks around the front and opens the passenger side door. Alley looks at her as if to seek permission. I swear, this lady has some sort of dog superpower. She looks at Alley, nods, and then my best friend bounds out of the car and jumps on me, planting her front paws on my chest to say hello. Having someone who makes me this happy whenever she sees me feels so much more than good. I ruffle the fur on her head and show her my love with a giant hug. Mrs. James clears her throat, and I reluctantly turn my attention toward her.

"The procedure went well. Alley is now fixed and fully compliant with AKC Guidelines and State Requirements. The vet will remove her sutures in two weeks, and she must wear the cone until then."

Turning my head slightly to the side and squinting a questioning eye, I try to figure out what the hell AKC means. This woman must be a fucking magician because somehow, she instantly read my thoughts.

"The American Kennel Club...for the love of all things dog. Doesn't ring a bell?"

I stare at her like a lost tourist without the camera. Shaking her head, she chuckles, leaving me wondering whether I amuse or annoy her with my dog ignorance. She goes back to her car and returns with her purse. Opening the clasp and reaching inside, I'm taken aback for a second when a thought pops into my head.

I hope she doesn't have a gun.

But when she pulls out a few sheets of folded paper, the notion of any forthcoming danger instantly goes away.

"These are the bills for the services rendered. Please, Guy, pay for them right away. Since I know most of the employees there, not paying, just would not do!"

She hands me the papers, and I assure her I will pay my bill today. Looking at me momentarily, she grins and then returns to her car.

"Guy, you need to eat, my boy. You look terrible. You must be drinking too much! Why don't you go look in the mirror and see the god-awful state you are in?"

I nod yes and smile, knowing it will take a lot more than a healthy meal to fix my problems. I raise my hand to my head and touch the cut above my eye, illustrating to her I get the point. She tsks at me, gets into her car, and turns on the engine. I notice that she still has a slight smile as she drives away. There is something different about this woman, her motherly ways and intriguing attitude, or whatever it is. I have yet to figure her out.

Alley heads to the stairwell, and I realize how lucky I am to share my space with her and have her as my friend.

One of my goals has always been to travel light, but lately, I have reconsidered. The desire for a connection or the responsibility of owning, caring for, and loving a dog or even being in a relationship has to be pre-ordained on some sub-conscious level. Then again, it could be something I desperately needed. I follow her to the door and open it, and she immediately hunts down Mr. Pig.

She cracks me up.

At first, I thought she would play aggressively with her toys, but she is so gentle with Mr. Pig and treats him like her baby. I love the contradiction displayed by this fine dog. I have seen her in stressful and quiet situations, and her duality or range is impressive. She's the gentlest soul with three-inch-long canine teeth. What was that old saying?

Walk softly and carry a big stick.

My mind turns back to Avery, and anxiety sets in. I'm nervous as I call to check on her status. Overwhelmed by the heavy guilt and the stress of this situation, I feel floods of emotion attacking me in all the wrong places. I call Aria, and I struggle to keep my hand from shaking while holding my phone. She picks up, and I instantly hear the fear, distress, and apprehension in her voice and tell her I'm on my way. Quickly, I gather a few things, toss them into my backpack, and leave. Of course, I bring Alley, my constant companion and shadow.

I request a ride and wait impatiently, pacing as Alley watches, confused or amused. I don't know which. My mind is on other things threatening to shatter what lies deep within me. It's because of me my friends are hurt, and if Avery dies, Aria will be destroyed. I have heard that twins have a special connection, and I don't want to see what happens if that bond is broken. I keep wishing it was me and that I could absorb their pain and hurt like a sin eater, someone deserving of punishment. It wouldn't be the worst thing I'd ever felt. My mind rages, and I quickly tense up as I circle the pavement, dwelling over my guilt. I don't notice this, but Alley sure does. She senses something is off, and she comes over to me, jumps up, and lands a big, sloppy tongue on my cheek. Her front paws press against my chest as she stands on her two back legs. Licking my face, she gets my attention, and it breaks my short-circuiting thoughts, giving me one more reason to love this amazing dog of mine.

I suddenly stop, shocked by that thought. When was the last time I could say I loved anything or anyone? The feeling is powerful and confusing, new to me and my little heart of stone. I rub Alley's head, ruffling her fur and her floppy ears. Lost in thought, I reflect upon the good things as I attempt to clear my mind of the distractions that continually haunt me. I need to snap out of this and pull myself together. My emotions are multiplying and running amuck within my brain. That is never good for anyone, but it's a warning sign for me.

As I think about Avery and Aria, I envision how I would feel if something happened to Alley, and I lost her. She has been the best thing to come into my life for a long time, and the thought of losing her sends an icy chill throughout my entire system.

Shake it off and turn the page.

I should invest in stock with this ride-share company because I hired yet another one today. It's like rolling the dice for me with whoever I get.

Some are just whack-a-mole, seriously.

I'm increasingly agitated, and my stomach feels queasy as I wait for my current chariot to arrive. Panic and tension set in because I know it's my fault. I feel an agonizing pain shoot through my heart, derailing my thoughts. I'm desperate and more than concerned about my friend's well-being.

I can't lose another!

I think of Aria, and instantly, remorse takes over. At that moment, right then, I vow to be there for her and keep her safe. I hear the music of my ride approach before I see it, and when it rounds the corner, I flag him down. Rap music booms from the car as it bumps into a sloppy stop before me.

Fuck it, who am I to judge?

I hop in the front seat, Alley jumping behind into the back as the young, black, twenty-something kid wearing a colorful patterned suit introduces himself.

"My man, I'm Clive Duvwaa...that's with two A's!"

He then laughs wildly, like Morris Day and the Time. After I shut the door, we bump fists and we're off and on our way to the hospital, as he continues.

"Bro, I'm your guy!"

Well, I'm Guy, bro.

I laugh a little at this, but he's persistent and continues rambling on, his voice flowing at full force without ever becoming weaker.

"I gotcha back. Whatcha need? Whatcha looking for? Whatcha into? Whatever it is, my man, I gotcha covered. Clive Duvwaa's got the hookup for every taste."

I look at the young entrepreneur and applaud his enthusiasm...slightly. I admire someone who wants more, is driven, is hungry, and works their ass off for it. Building a business is so much more than a hustle. He hands me an old-school business card, and I slip it into my pocket. Clive continues his presentation, attempting to grab a potential sale or customer while vending me on his services, connections, and talents as we drive.

Arriving at the hospital, he pulls to the front, and I thank Mr. Clive Duvwaa before he booms away, the bass rattling the windows as he passes. Alley turns her head, looking back in aversion, and I can tell she doesn't like the loud pounding noise.

I rush into the hospital with my sidekick, my palms sweaty from the thoughts raging around in my tormented mind. I find Aria, and her tear-stained face breaks my heart in two as she looks lifelessly straight through my diminishing soul. I rush over to her and wrap my arms around her petite frame, and she cries into my chest. I feel her hot breath and the wetness of her tears through my shirt, scorching my front with the fire from the flames of guilt, responsibility, and shame.

I caused this, or at least I didn't stop it.

What good are these skills if I can't use them to save the ones I hold dear?

I hold Aria as she weeps for what seems like forever but is only five minutes. Her eyes are the reddest I have ever seen as she breaks away from my embrace. She looks at me questioningly, and I feel blank and devoid of answers or the right words to say. Aria stoops, and I introduce her to Alley. As she sadly pets my companion, she looks up at me with a river of tears rolling down her face.

"Why did this happen, Guy? Why? Who?"

I can tell that her mind is racing, the wheels are spinning, and I assure her we will get to the bottom of all that, but right now, we need to be strong for Avery. Distracting her momentarily, we find a high-tech vending machine and get a weird little cup of infamous hospital coffee.

As we stretch our legs and pace the floor, I tell Aria everything I know about this situation. Alley is always close by, and the hospital staff look questioningly but move on as she lies calmly and peacefully by a chair. Aria's only operating on about 30% right now, but she's still the most intelligent person in the room and proves it once again as she abruptly makes a connection.

"Svetlana knows the code, or at least where to find it. I'm sure of it."

A solemn doctor unexpectedly interrupts us, and my heart skips a beat, then drops into the pit of my stomach.

Please, God, no!

Aria turns and looks toward the doctor, her eyes tearing up again. I see the color drain from her face, and she hyperventilates. Alley lifts her chin, perking her ears up.

"Ms. Storm, I'm so deeply sorry. We tried everything we could, but the damage was severe and irreparable. She fought..."

Instantly, time seems warped, and as the air goes still, I hear nothing else. I grab Aria, now an orphan whose other half was erased by a callous act of violence. Her body collapses, and I lift her, holding her upright.

Why is this world so fucked up and cruel?

Why do people need to be such fucking dark stains on the clean white slate of the innocent?

Tears burn down my cheeks, but I know it's nothing compared to Aria's pain.

That sounds like the title of a sad classical music song.

We're in the middle of the hallway, and I'm still hugging her tightly, keeping the pieces of my friend together. She has a thousand-yard stare, and I can see her fighting the reality of this truly fucked up situation. Her life is changing, and she can't stop this chapter from ever closing. A nurse brings her a mild sedative, and Aria takes the pills without even looking or asking what they are.

Please don't break, Aria.

We walk from the hall into the hospital, and I feel like I have left a piece of myself behind. I don't know if the doctors or nurses need us anymore, but we have to go. The further we walk, the more I feel the weight. Alley follows behind with a worried look on her face. She senses something terrible has happened and looks between us with sympathy only the pure can genuinely express.

I look over at Aria and see her shuffling her feet stiffly as she conceals her cries. Gently, I steer her by the shoulder as we walk out in silence. She can't see clearly through her blurry eyes and tears, but we eventually make it outside. She fumbles with her dark sunglasses as I get us a ride. I hold my phone and stare at the screen.

What happened? How? This doesn't feel real!

I feel like I'm going to snap under the ever-increasing pressure on my chest. I want to cry. I want to punch something. I want to rage against this fucked up world and the evil bullshit that lives within its shadows. The cold, dark places where the righteous suffer and the wicked play, reveling in the anonymity of a cold and cruel universe.

I push the thoughts of snow away, but it's getting harder to forget the flames. I feel heat so scorching it's like a cold, searing certainty, and I know that before this day is over, there will be much more blood and death.

A reckoning is coming, and the pieces of this puzzle will be put together.

I eventually get a ride, and our car shows up much quicker than expected. My gut tells me something isn't right. It seems squirrelly, but my bandwidth is full of today's distractions. I'm hurting, and my intuitive nature is on vacation. When I enter the vehicle, I immediately notice Jenny sitting in the passenger seat and holding a gun. I know I'm fucked when a hurried man hops in from the other side and leans toward me.

"Run Aria!"

Startled, Aria sprints away immediately, running on instinct more than anything else. Alley looks at me. She's startled and confused as I tell her I love her and slam the door behind me, protecting her from the trap. She can't help me right now, and I can't put anyone else I care for in danger. She barks at the car, clearly panic-stricken.

The driver looks at Jenny, who nods her head, and he slowly drives away. The man sitting next to me shoves a pistol into my ribcage as he slips a hood over my head. Even though this current predicament has me in quite a bind, I'm holding on to the guilt I feel and can't stop thinking about Avery.

Goodbye, Avery. You deserved better than this. I promise you, they will pay.

Chapter Nineteen

Run Aria!

I hear Guy yell for me to run, and something in his voice moves me before I can even process why. My fight-or-flight kicks in, and I'm gone like the wind. Usually I'm a little spacey, but I feel positively displaced right now. So much has happened and is still happening. My head spins, consumed by the memory of what I have just experienced, and all I can think about is the one thing that made me whole.

Avery.

My beautiful twin...my better half.

I feel like a shadow without a body...incomplete.

I can't believe this is happening. As I'm running, I pretend she's still here—still alive. The sun is beating down upon me like an incandescent bulb hung in an interrogation room, burning away the lie. The morning is already getting hot as I run down the sidewalk. Tears are rolling down my cheeks, and for me, the world is a confusing and blurry kaleidoscope of emotions.

I don't know where I'm going, and I let my feet lead me as my mind drifts a thousand miles away in a sea of unfathomable pain. I don't know how to be without her.

Oh, Avery! Why not me?

I bump into people as I stumble down the street, absorbed in my pain. Every stranger I knock against somehow reminds me that this situation with Avery is unbelievably cruel and unfair. I'm furious with Avery's killers and frustrated at the universe. I'm angry at life...at Guy... at myself. I want to rage at the injustice of it all.

I'm tired of this painful life...so useless... I just wish I could die.

The thought shocks me...but I'm out of control... I want to self-destruct.

What's the point?

Then a thought slams into my mind. Avery...I know she would never give up. If the situation was reversed, she would be after my killers already, weapon in hand.

Why am I so weak?

I struggle mentally with this as I walk, chastising myself for my failure to my twin. Possibly, I might find peace if I discover why they stole her life.

I wish Avery was here to ask her opinion.

The sun seems much brighter than it should be, and I worry I might get a migraine. I need to figure out where to go because I can't go home—not yet. I'm not ready to walk in and see all of Avery's belongings, and no Avery.

I'll need to pack up her things.

The thought rips me apart, and I need to find a place to process it. I hire a ride-share, and soon, I'm on my way to the same hotel where I was supposed to meet Guy. I figure that's as good a place as any to hole up in, and maybe then I might figure out more about what was going on.

And cry...cry so hard that my eyes bleed.

Chapter Twenty

At the same time Aria is heading to the hotel, Alley is running down a side street, scared and confused. She knows something terrible has happened. She rubs against a building's sharp edge, and the cone around her neck falls to the ground.

She loves her new pack and den. She had just started to get used to it. She runs on instinct and heads back to her old stomping grounds. She knows how to survive out there. It's just that she didn't think she would have to live like that anymore.

As she runs, the wind moves her fur, and her stride flexes her powerful muscles, waking the genetic lineage of wolves in her DNA. She dodges across the street, slightly leery of the cars and trucks that speed past her. She runs along the sidewalk and leaps effortlessly over obstacles, skillfully weaving through the people who walk in every direction.

She turns down a side alley and scares away a cat snooping around a dumpster, sending it hissing and scampering away. The scent in the air is getting familiar, and Alley hopes to see her pack Alpha again. She looks for him in the same spot where she first found him. As she passes the back door of a restaurant, a cook is bringing out some garbage. He sees Alley and shouts at her.

"Get out of here, you rabid stray!"

She's heard that sound before, and plenty of hostility always accompanied it. Typically, she would have shied away, but her Alpha showed her she didn't have to be so timid. She bared her teeth and gave this human a preview of what would happen if he didn't submit. Alley growled low and deep and scared the man. The chef's eyes got big, and as he dropped the garbage, he called over his shoulder for his co-worker to help.

"Simon! Call animal control! We have a wild stray back here! This city is going to hell!"

She hears that sound again and barks, showing the man she knows how to make threatening sounds too. She barks at him several times before he can shuffle his way back inside the restaurant.

Why is this happening?

Alley feels scared and she thinks she has done something wrong. Had she been kicked out of the pack? The thought makes her lower her head. She whines for a bit and then fights off the tears that are forming.

Alley had been sitting outside for a while, feeling lost and confused. She's gentle and skittish for a big dog. All she had ever wanted was to be loved and to belong.

Where's my pack? Where is my Alpha?

As she thinks her dog thoughts, she doesn't notice the loop slowly approaching behind her on a pole. It brushes her ear, but as she jerks away, it's too late. The noose tightens around her neck, and panic sets in instantly. She attempts to yelp but can't as it's lifting her by the neck, bringing her front legs off the ground. She twists and turns to no avail. She sees the human holding the pole, fighting to control her. He moves slowly as he backs her up to a truck with cages. Alley doesn't want to go and fights the entire way, not giving in until she can't breathe.

The human lets Alley catch her breath and then uses the lull to force her into the back of his Animal Control truck. He slams the cage door and bends over, hands on his knees, catching his breath.

"Sorry, buddy. You're a fighter, but I have a job to do. Let's get you to your new home."

He gets back into his vehicle, and moments later, Alley feels it move. She panics as she circles the locked area, and when the driver hits a huge dip in the road, she curls up as small as she can in the corner, whimpering with her ears down and more afraid than she's ever been.

I just want to go home.

Chapter Twenty-One

As Alley is thinking about that bleak thought, Aria arrives at the hotel Guy wanted to meet at. She walks inside and through the lobby toward the elevators.

Avery...

I wonder if yesterday she walked where I'm walking now.

I miss her so much that I look for anything that will connect me to her. I enter the elevator, push the button, and keep my finger on it ever so lightly.

Had she touched this?

I ride the elevator up, lost in gloomy thoughts of unlikely connections. I exit and soon find myself standing outside the hotel room door.

What if Guy checked out and someone else was here?

I have to wing it and knock before I lose my nerve. I'm a total wreck right now. The door opens, and a beautiful woman wearing a silky robe stands before me. She looks annoyed, but then her expression turns to concern. I manage to get a few words out.

"Uh...Guy... Guy... oh... my sister!"

I burst into tears right there in the hallway in front of this stranger. I register none of this, as my pain has already taken me to an entirely different place. I feel like I'm falling as the woman guides me inside before shutting the door. She puts her arm around me and steers me into the little front area.

As we pass a mirror, I catch a glimpse of myself. My eyes are red with dark circles under them, and my mascara is running like a high school breakup face - blotchy and pale.

I look a hundred years older.

She tuts at me like an old Russian nana, and I find the simple act endearing and slightly helpful. I sit on the couch, and this kind stranger goes to the minibar, returning with a handful of bottles.

"I'm not sure what you drink, but you look like you need something."

I take a random bottle from her and crack open the top.

"Are you Svetlana?"

She looks briefly shocked, and then her hand flies to her mouth.

"Guy..."

I gulp down the tiny bottle of vodka and instantly regret it. My stomach lurches, and I fight not to vomit. I squeeze my eyes shut...like that's going to help. I'm trying to grieve...to self-destruct.

Isn't this what I'm supposed to do?

"Who are you?"

Svetlana asks me this guarded and pulls her robe tighter on her body. She then remembers that Guy had called his nerd friend to meet them there.

"You are...Cornflake?"

I smile at the nickname and introduce myself.

"Yes, Svetlana. My name is Aria. I grew up with Guy and sometimes help him with tech stuff. I'm sorry. None of that matters right now. I saw Guy get kidnapped about an hour ago, when we were leaving the hospital, after my sister had just died."

I can't hold back the tears at this thought, so I cry again. I will never look at that hospital the same. I then remember the car and ask Svetlana for some paper and a pen. She walks across the room to retrieve them for me. I squeeze my eyes tightly as I try to envision the details.

Come on, Aria, think!

She brings me a hotel notepad and a pen, and I write down everything I can remember about the car and the few moments right after. I make a list of a few things which help other details emerge. I'm soon looking at a detailed description of the car and the most significant information.

The license plate number.

I realize this is slightly helping with my grief and continue trying to remember any other details.

Alley!

I'm so messed up with my situation that I forgot about Alley, Guy's dog. What happened to her? It went down so fast; I didn't see where she ran off to. I need to find her for Guy. Plus, she has sutures and a cone around her neck.

I notice Guy's laptop sitting on the desk. I'm talking with Svetlana as I get up from the couch and make my way over to the desk.

"We have to locate Guy's dog, Alley."

I open the laptop, type in Guy's password, and I'm online. I wrack my brain for ideas as I'm checking his email. I find it depressing that Guy receives such a small handful, but I quickly find a recent one from Eleanore James with the subject line: Castle, Alley. I notice Alley's chip ID number at the bottom after reading a lengthy diatribe on the neglect of animals and how to care for a dog properly.

Now we are cooking!

Chapter Twenty-Two

Meanwhile, feeling abandoned, a sad Alley is curled up in the corner of a cold and dirty kennel. To top it off, she misses her Mr. Pig. Time continues to turn with the planet, and all Alley wanted was to be loved and to belong.

Why am I never good enough?

Stray!

Whimpering moans of hopelessness and despair rang repeatedly as the depressing sounds bounced off the walls and echoed throughout the building. No, she refused to cave. Alley had felt loved and had a genuine connection with her Alpha. She knew she belonged, and that she was part of the pack. Alley got up and paced the kennel, worried. How will they find me? The thought momentarily breaks the wailing noises of the lost and forgotten.

Stray!

Alley raises her snout and lets out a low and sad howl. The other dogs there that still feel a connection to their past join in, and it's the most heartbreaking song. The young women working in another kennel area look up and then at each other as they bear witness to this pain-laden requiem. All they wanted was to be loved and belong, but this world is cold.

Ding!

One of the young kennel workers heads to the front lobby through the far door, locking it behind. After a few minutes, the door opens again, and Alley catches the familiar scents. She perks up her ears, listening to the footsteps, and as they get closer, she becomes more excited. Alley lifts her head when they stop in front of the kennel cage door. She recognizes the two women who stand before her.

Her pack!

Her tail wags when she rushes to the cage door, and once there, she lets out the most joyful bark.

What took you so long?

She's ready to leave. Svetlana stoops and scratches Alley behind the ears, ruffling her fur lovingly. Aria pays with Guy's card, and Alley gets released from the clink about five minutes later.

Alley leads the way out with her tail swishing rapidly as they exit the facility. It's a sad place, but it reunited Alley and her pack, so it's just another example of how complex this world is.

Aria and Svetlana discuss their next move while waiting for their latest ride share. Alley stands by their side and sniffs the air, looking for her Alpha. They head back to the hotel and regroup. When the ride shows up, it's a cute twenty-something guy. Svetlana eagerly hops in the front seat while Alley and Aria jump in the back. As they drive, Svetlana and the cute guy flirt back and forth. Aria stares out the back window, lost in her sad thoughts. Alley senses Aria's pain and lays her head on Aria's lap.

You are not alone, Aria.

When the girls arrive at the hotel, they quickly head to the room. In the elevator, Aria remembers her notes from earlier when she brain-dumped right after she got to the hotel room. She unfolds the hotel stationery and reads over it again. She follows Svetlana as they walk to their room, lost in thought. She stares at the paper, Alley bringing up the rear.

Aria heads directly to the laptop when they enter the hotel room and flips it open. As the familiar electric light illuminates her face, her wheels are already turning. How is she going to do this? How is she going to find Guy? She has a weird feeling that Avery was sitting on the couch watching her, and she has to look over at it to dispel the feeling. She refocuses her attention and holds the outside pain at bay.

She knows this distraction is a mirage, but the pain feels like a mountain balanced above her head right now, and there are shadows as far as she can see. Her fingers fly across the keyboard as she hacks into the Masserro County Motor Vehicle Database. She cross-references the plate number and car description and returns with a hit.

Bingo!

"I found the car!"

As Svetlana exits the bedroom, she inquires.

"How are we going to do this? We can't use a ride-share."

Svetlana has a point, and Aria nods, trying to solve the problem. She begins pacing back and forth while Alley watches curiously from the couch that has become her new perch. Aria then heads over to the laptop, accesses Guy's email again, and pulls up the message from Mrs. Eleanore James with the subject line: Castle, Alley. Contact information was at the bottom of the message, and Aria writes it on her notes.

I sure hope she's a friend.

Aria and Svetlana exchange looks as Svetlana dials the number on her phone and puts it on speaker. After it rings twice, it connects.

"Hello?"

The women look at each other, and Aria finally speaks. Svetlana shakes her head.

"Hello, is this Mrs. Eleanore James?"

"Yes, how may I help you, dear?"

"We have a mutual friend...Guy Castle? He's in trouble, and we need your help."

Mrs. James gasps before she replies.

"Oh my! Is he ok, Miss?"

"My name is Aria Storm, Ma'am, but we're not sure. "

"What is it, Miss Storm, that you need my help with?"

"We know where we need to rescue Guy from, but we need a discrete driver and a vehicle."

"I also believe time is of the essence."

Aria says the last part out of stress and frustration as the day's emotions stack up again. She takes a deep breath before continuing.

"He was kidnapped this morning, and I don't know why."

Aria's emotions get the best of her, and she struggles to keep it together. Svetlana sees this and steps in for her newfound friend.

"Will you be able to help us, Mrs. James?"

"Who is this now that I'm speaking to?"

Svetlana rolls her eyes and replies as if it was the stupidest question in the world.

"Svetlana...Patinko."

"Well, Mrs. Patinko, why don't you call the police? This certainly sounds like a crime has been committed."

"The police are useless, and we need to help him now. They will take too long. So again, I ask you, Mrs. James...will you help us?"

"Well, of course, dear, where are you? I will be right over."

"Thank you, Mrs. James. We're at the Four Seasons."

Chapter Twenty-Three

The name still cracked her up, Nora James, the whole thing really. Eleanore, or Nora, as her friends called her, was born with a different name. Nora was born Sandy Sherman and grew up on the meaner streets of Cincinnati, Ohio. As a teenager, Sandy found she liked the rush of living a danger-ous lifestyle and surfed the edge with luck far longer than most. As her luck continued, her false sense of security grew. Soon, Sandy was running with shady people and became a witness to some dangerous and frightening things. It was too late when she realized there was no escape, and the stakes were stacked too high.

One rainy night, while she was with some others at the port of Cincinnati, Sandy witnessed something that became too much, and she needed to find a way out. In a shadowy corner of the shipping yard where only rats play, a container full of human prisoners was being opened, and the scene was absolute carnage. The smell was overwhelming, and the ones that were still alive inside wandered out like zombies, emaciated and dehydrated. The sight of a little arm, pale, and limp, laying just so under the weak sodium lighting broke her.

She had never been a traitor nor a snitch, but there are some lines that nobody should cross. When they are crossed, all bets and loyalties are gone. It's on that person who made that decision to do the unspeakable. Fuck them if they dislike being dragged out of their slimy, dark, secret caves and into the light. Sandy never enjoyed being pushed around and never aspired to be a part of what she was dragged into. Her common sense told her that the sooner she went to the police for help, the sooner it would be over and look better for her.

It was difficult the first time she entered the police station; it was the hardest. She was honest with them, as she had nothing to hide and went along with their undercover sting operation. When immunity and witness protection became an option for full cooperation, Sandy became the star witness in a case with far-reaching consequences. Many influential people fell because of their stupid greed and gray moral thinking. Sandy Sherman went into the program and was reborn a completely different person, Mrs. Eleanore James.

Well, Sandy liked dogs, too.

The thought of all this cracks her up again as she finishes putting the little pink snub-nosed revolver into her designer purse. Because you never know. She goes to the board hung by the door and grabs the *"other"* keys.

Moments later, a throaty roar starts, and a midnight blue 1967 Shelby GT500 rolls out of her garage with a well-oiled purr. This is her baby, and she does all the mechanical work herself. It started as something she could do to feel closer to her late dad and grew into a personal passion project.

Despite her outward demeanor, Nora is worried about Guy. When she first met him, she saw right through his bravado, but admired his tenacity. It's hard to find a man nowadays with a spine, and her attitude changed dramatically toward him when it became apparent that he was helping a poor stray. He has a lot to learn about dogs, but she could tell he was a good man.

She has met enough bad ones to know the difference.

He's also very handsome, but she pushes that thought deep down and with a giggle.

When she pulls up to the front of the hotel, all three girls are waiting for her. As soon as she arrives, Alley starts barking and circling by her door, eager to see her.

"Alley! That's enough...sit!"

No sooner had the words left Nora's mouth and Alley's butt slams to the ground.

"Good girl. Now ladies, let's go get our Guy, if you would be so kind."

They pile into the souped-up Shelby, and the tires smoke as they tear out of the parking lot moments later. They are an unlikely group, but they share a worry for Guy and a common goal to save him.

Chapter Twenty-Four

A couple of minutes into my kidnap drive, I hear the man next to me speak.

"Goodnight, Guy!"

I'm hit with a powerful stun gun, and my world goes dark. I have no idea how long I've been out. I remember them having to stun me a few times, as I kept waking up throughout the long and torturous ride. When I finally come to, my body hurts from all the electric stings, and I breathe through the pain as my ragged nerves try to recover. My scrub top is ripped, hanging in shreds, and I find myself shivering in a cold, dank space. I wonder where I am, and then I have a moment of twisted clarity when I want to give up. This doesn't happen often, but when it does, I stop caring about everything and everyone in my life.

I'm in a world of shit right now, blowing like a hurricane...or a blizzard.

My mind is spinning with everything that has happened in the last two days. My body feels numb, and as my soul slips away heavily and falls through the floor, I wonder if it will ever return. My heart hurts to its core. I feel as though I'm being tortured and like I've lost everything, which is not too far from the truth. But I don't know why I was put in the middle of this nightmarish power struggle when I didn't even have a goddamn horse in the race. The more I try to escape my past, the more it gets in my face.

Oh my god...Avery!

Shame is burning like acid through my veins as the pain of my failure flows uneasily throughout my body, consuming every cell - one by one. Avery would still be alive if I hadn't involved her. The rage I feel helps me loosen my binds and, by violently rocking my chair, I crash down onto the cold concrete floor. I lay there motionless with my cheek against the blood-speckled cement, my wrists going numb from my bindings.

The door opens, and I glance at a wooden stairway leading up. A man enters, and I instantly recognize him as the one sitting next to me in the car. He has medium-length, shaggy blond hair, and a handlebar mustache, with a style that has me calling him "Boogie Nights." Striding across the floor, the guy dips down, grabs my chair, and easily swings it upward. This shows me that his solid, muscular body is not just for looks or attention. Then, with a noncommittal grin, he sucker punches me in the nose, leaving it bloody and tilted toward the left side of my face.

Not even a kiss before he fucked me over.

My eyes instantly water as the cold sinus shock shoots through my head, radiating a growing pain-like fire from my face outward. I feel lit sparklers right behind my eyes, and it makes me nauseous for a second as blood pours from my nose. He hits me a few times in the stomach, more rabbit jabs than anything powerful, and then backs up. I gasp, trying to catch my breath.

"Hey, tough guy, why don't you untie me?"

I can see he's enjoying the temporary control he holds over me.

"Give us what we want, and maybe I will?"

I've known shitbags like this disco ball my whole life, bullies and thugs who prey on the weak to make themselves feel powerful.

I joined the Army to even that score...I hate bullies!

"Give you what? The number to a good psychologist? When I'm done with you, Boogie Nights, you'll need a lot more help than that."

He smiles at this, shaking his head in surprise before continuing.

"Your good psychologist doesn't seem to be working for you."

He retorts, and I silently have to agree with him.

"You're a real hard case, huh?"

He lunges in quickly and punches me smack in the mouth. I feel pain shoot from my lip as it splits against my teeth. My mouth fills with blood, joining my nose, and I spit it out, covering myself in my own gore. He hits me again in the eye socket, and I see my white stars for a split second before they dissolve into black.

When I regain consciousness, my head is bowed, and a long, bloody train of drool is traveling down my chin and onto my pecs. I keep my eyes closed and listen carefully with intent, trying to get any sort of intel. Some of my teeth feel loose, and I mess with them slightly with my tongue, checking each one.

I hear faint voices coming from above and footsteps nearing the room. I listen to the plod of each foot, which tells me that two people are coming down the stairs.

"He's awake!"

When I hear this, I realize I'm not being as sneaky as I thought.

Opening my eyes, I notice that blood has dripped down my chest and is covering the dog tags around my neck. Then, without fail, my mind is taken back to a time I find difficult to bury. As my memory recreates the scenes, I envision that horrendous and deadly experience that stings painfully into every cell of my body. Raising my head, I see that Jenny's standing there. She looks at me with pure hatred, and I'm confused.

Why are you doing this?

"Why don't you recognize me? Not from Charlie's but from before."

I look at her again and know that something is rattling around in this warped brain of mine, but I still can't place her. It doesn't help that Boogie Nights has been throwing a disco in my head, playing songs of torture and pain.

Fuck you, pal!

Looking offended, she gets my attention again as she stalks back and forth in front of me like a tiger hungrily eyeing up its meal. A cold shiver shoots up my spine, and every hair on my body instantly stands at attention. The woman is lit from above by a bright and unflattering incandescent bulb that slowly sways every time she moves. Her shadows graze across the floor like a hidden dance. Boogie Nights comes in for another punch, and his fist hits the light, causing it to swing erratically. The room seems to spin with dark violence, and at haphazard angles, a lightning pain cuts through me.

The blow feels like electricity as he smacks my ear with his fisted hand, and as the light staggers around the room, causing shadows to waltz dramatically, he rains down upon me in a storm of blows. My body feels numb from the constant abuse, and I grunt through the pain of each whack.

"Enough!"

The woman yells this with authority, and Mr. Mustache backs off. I spit blood at him, grinning as my eye swells shut. She rushes toward me and slams a picture against my burning flesh. It falls to my lap, and the sight of it hits me harder than anything I have endured today. I look back at the woman, and she gives me a sad smile.

The picture shows a young happy couple on their wedding day. She looks beautiful, excited, and so in love as she stands next to...

...oh my God, Frank.

My blood-covered dog tags burn against my chest as one of them has a lot more significance right now. She's the widow of Doc, one of the teammates I lost on that nightmare of a mission ten years ago.

The horrible night my ghosts were born.

I can't stop the barrage of memories, which rush combatively into my mind and spread throughout my entire body, weighing heavily on my cold and empty soul. I remember fire and snow.

Our eyes lock, and a tear falls from the lower lid of her piercing gaze, dragging her mascara down with it. I'm speechless as she walks away and disappears up the stairs. I want to explain. No, I need to explain. I want to tell her how I was punished and blamed for something I couldn't prevent! I desperately need her to believe me.

Please!

As I'm thinking this, Boogie Nights pistol-whips me, and it's lights out once again.

Chapter Twenty-Five

Guy sits in the dark, still strapped to the chair. As he comes to, he's confused about where he is and what happened. His whole body feels both empty and full of pain as he's having a tough time processing this.

What the fuck just happened? How did I...

It all starts returning to me as I regain consciousness, like slowly emerging from oil. It's like my mind is playing my memories backward. My chest is crusty and wet with my drool and blood as I slowly move around, flexing against my binds.

Doc!

Doc's widow looked so mad, and mustache? Who is he?

Oh yeah, Boogie Nights! That motherfucker is going to die, I promise myself.

With that thought, my eyes open instantly, and I scan around my area, again in control of all my faculties. It's more like just one eye, as the other is swollen shut, and my cheek throbs underneath. I can feel wet drool on my face and stringing along my chest.

Where am I?

I slowly crane my neck around as I take in my dark environment. There is a door in front of me, and I remember I saw stairs behind...leading up. I rock my chair, and it moves freely.

Amateurs.

I look at the ground and see again the wedding picture of the happy young couple. I know Mustache is going to die, but I don't want to hurt Doc's widow. We all do crazy shit sometimes, and I can't imagine the loss she must feel. I had a weird moment where I wondered if Doc was just whispering in my ear and decided I would take it. It's better than what my ghosts usually say to me.

As I wait there, the cold slowly seeps into my exposed flesh. I'm tired, and my whole-body hurts. I'm also registering a light dizziness feeling that I know all too well.

I'm losing too much blood.

The world slowly slips back into the dark oil, and I wonder if I'll recover from this or finally join my ghosts.

The room is fading white, and I see fire and death everywhere. The snow is blowing so hard that my vision is impaired, and if I turn my head directly towards it, I know the wind will take my breath away.

We were so new.

A team formed barely a year ago. I'm concerned about my mission as I look around, remembering the details as if they had just happened.

Where did I put my map?

"Rodeo, this is Whiskey 3 coms check, over."

"Whiskey 3, this is Rodeo. We read you Lima Charlie, how me? Over."

"Rodeo, Whiskey 3...we read you same. Will update with anything new at next check in, Whiskey 3 out."

I heard the team's radio man, Staff Sergeant Edward Johnson, complete the latest radio check as I surveyed our mission environment. He's the newest member of this freshly formed team and fits in great. Johnson knows his stuff. The storm has kicked up, and the visibility is dropping rapidly. I adjust the weight of my pack, rocking it up and towards my back as I hold the shoulder straps. I ache, but it's part of the job, and I don't even register it anymore. It helps when there are bigger things to worry about, and right now, there are.

Intel was tracking a known anarchist and terrorist leader who was also of extreme interest to about eight countries and about every other law enforcement agency. This person's name is a mystery; he or she is only known as the Sparrow. He or she was on a plane somewhere within this grid and had disappeared less than fourteen hours before.

Whiskey is a newer team that has been operating together ad hoc for a little under a year as part of a larger NATO HUMINT sharing program. Everyone here is eager to meet each other's families when our current rotation is over. We have gelled through the experiences shared over the last year, and we are looking forward to enjoying the simple life together with our families.

The special operations community is small and tight, and we watch out for our own. I look at my fellow warriors and see a future of weddings, funerals, christenings, and baptisms, practical jokes, and shared heartbreak. This life is hard and not meant for the weak or non-committed. Special Ops is a life, not a job, and certainly not a joke. When you operate in a hurricane, you need something strong to ground you.

If you lose that, you're lost.

We've set up a listening and observation position atop a dominating land feature and are checking our search grid progress. Two days ago, we found parts of the wreckage of the plane but no bodies. The continual snowfall and the back-to-back high-speed gusts of wind had eliminated all tracks and markings. Based on the terrain angle and slope, it's a good guess that the Sparrow would have walked downhill or east. We narrow down the search grid, temporarily attempting to locate the person or, at a very minimum, the body.

"Johnson, how's the signal?"

Like all great team medics, our team medic, Frank, has the original nickname Doc, which is purely given out of respect. Naval Corpsman Petty Officer First Class Frank Carpenter adjusts his weapon as he rotates his neck, working out the kinks from the long two-day trek to get here. This alpine environment is as rugged as it comes, and the movement has been slow.

"Five by five, Doc. You got anything to help with this cold bullshit?"

"Nothing that won't melt a cup, bro."

Doc jokes, but I can tell he's silently going through his medical inventory and different situations in his head. He stays ready, and he's as loyal as they come. He has already pulled a few pieces of metal out of me and a piece of someone else's bone.

That is a story I don't intend to tell.

In my book, he's a solid, honest man, and I'm proud to serve with him.

I'm proud to serve with all of them.

The last man on our team is a woman. Her name is Jessica Townsand. She's a staff sergeant, Sapper qualified, and a team engineer. She's tougher than most other operators I know and works twice as hard to silence the misogyny she experiences from time to time within the community. There will be an awakening when her story gets out and heard.

I guarantee that shit will stop.

She's a true operator, and I would hate to experience her scorn. Her call sign is Reaper and for a reason.

She's checking the map confirming our location against the GPS. Scanning the immediate area, I look around, more out of habit than necessity. I never mind going out on snowy missions because I always enjoyed the silence. Of course, until things kick off, and then it's always the same old song.

We have been using snowshoes and making good time. I pulled the LP/OP and move before the weather worsens. We quickly gather our things, tightening straps and arranging the weight. Reaper has some pogey bait that she pulls out to share, giving us some quick fuel as we set off on our hunt for the Sparrow.

The snow drifts through the trees like thin sheets of silence, and the calm is broken from time to time by a branch snapping under the weight of the snow. I took point and stealthily led us through the trees, pausing often to listen and scan our surroundings. This is a methodical dance mixed with chess moves, not a leisurely stroll in the woods. The Sparrow is not to be underestimated, and the fact that we are tracking this person instead of law enforcement speaks volumes.

I catch movement ahead and to the left, and I hold my fist in the air, signaling the team to freeze. We sink down and wait. I know from the map that a road is close, and I see a vehicle pass. I point forward twice, then move my palm straight down, signaling for us to approach cautiously. We slowly move closer to the road and then wait, listening and studying the immediate area. When another vehicle approaches us, we silently melt back into the icy shadows again.

As the truck passes, we see it belongs to a civilian military contractor named JP Green Tactical Solutions. We know these guys and have had problems with them in the past. We wait, and another vehicle passes, then another. I'm getting a sinking feeling in my gut that they're here to extract the Sparrow.

Dropping back into the woods again and circling up, we decide what to do next. We spool up our satellite imaging pad and see a collection of vehicles parked together in a closed campground about half-a-mile north of us. We set off smoothly toward our target, gliding silently over the snow like ghosts.

We observe while carefully listening when we arrive at the target area's periphery. Men in mismatched gear and black BDU-style uniforms are milling around the trucks. Some look like they're guarding and patrol the area, but mostly, there's a lot of grab-assing going on. These "professionals" look like they're waiting, doing a quick size-up. I count five trucks and twenty men. Even for us, that is a little heavy, and I wish upon a star for a missile launcher.

Well, what was that old saying?

Wish in one hand, shit in the other, see which one...something?

Honestly, I never got that analogy, but right now, that hand with shit is making a big old sandwich for us, and I just brushed my teeth. I'm in the middle of another deep thought when I see one mercenary heading in our direction. He's taking his time, and I'm sure he's looking for a place to pee.

I'm silently willing him to fuck off the closer he gets. When he's about fifteen feet away, he shifts his gear weight and unbuttons his fly. He scans the area, pulling out his little soldier when our eyes meet.

Mine are squinting along my sights as his open wide in shock. I think the last thing going through his mind, besides my bullet, was absolute surprise. I had a silencer attached, but it was still loud enough to make some heads turn. We would slink back into the shadows, except they see their buddy fall.

"Contact!"

Tree branches start snapping and falling all around us as every gun lights up the area. As bullets snap past us, snow and pine needles rain down upon our heads. We low crawl away as quickly as possible down a rise, then get up and run. Bullets chase us down a draw, and I'm glad I don't hear dogs. We are sliding down the rocks and scree as quickly as possible, hearing shouts much closer than I would like. We hit the road and run down it, trying to gain some distance.

An old blue truck comes around the bend and slows to a stop in front of us. An older man with a beat-up John Deere hat looks at us with a slight grin as we approach his window.

"We being invaded?"

"No, sir, but we need your truck. It's an emergency."

He looks briefly shocked, then at the American flag patch on my shoulder. He gets out, shaking his head, and we pile in. Reaper jumps in the bed with Doc and apologizes for inconveniencing the man.

"We're sorry about this, sir."

I throw it in drive and hear him yell as we speed off.

"Don't be Troop, I was, and still am, a Marine...Semper fi!"

Chapter Twenty-Six

We would have called for help, but our radio took a hit and now only speaks sparking nonsense. We're going fast, and the roads are getting slicker as the snow piles up. The truck fishtails then corrects as we pull around a turn and barely miss a vehicle traveling in the opposite direction. They honk as we pass them, and I glance in the rear-view mirror before adjusting again as the truck slides. It's getting dark, and I throw on the headlights. They barely cut through the sheets of snow and are mesmerizing to look at as we speed through them.

I hear Reaper and Doc fire their weapons and glance at my side mirror. Like a dragon emerging from the smoke, the lead pursuer emerges in a dark-colored truck from the snowstorm. A moment later, the mirror shatters as a bullet passes through it.

That object was definitely closer than it appeared.

Someone's bullet hits the driver, and the truck veers violently to the side before flipping and rolling down the hill. It comes to a crunching stop straight into a massive tree.

We don't get to enjoy our victory for long, as another vehicle takes its place like a hungry wolf. They continue to fire out their windows, and bullets crack by us as we slip and slide along the road. The ground is piling up with snow, and it's hard to see in spots. Our luck runs out when bullets impact the truck's tail, sparking and ricocheting off at crazy angles. We slide, and I see a ditch coming up fast.

"Hold on!"

I get the tires to catch at the last second and at least get the truck so that it hits the ditch and slides into it to a grinding stop. The impact jars us with my head hitting the side window hard enough to break it, and I'm glad I'm wearing a helmet. I shake away the stars, and we pile out, bullets hitting around us.

Johnson grunts and drops instantly as a bullet takes his life. We're firing back at them reactively as we head for the tree line and stop when we see Johnson fall. Doc starts to run back to him, but I'd seen the lights go out when Johnson was struck.

"Doc, he's gone. Move your ass!"

I hear Doc curse, but training kicks in, and he lays down some fire before bounding back into the trees. I'm closest to Johnson, and I quickly yank his tags, almost taking a bullet in the process. This pisses me off, as some of these shitbirds used to serve. I turn around and empty a full clip, then another I had taken from Johnson's vest, killing everyone in the truck, including Johnson's killer.

I give him a few extra for Johnson. RIP Brother.

I see another truck sliding to a stop, and I throw a grenade into the first truck bed on my way past. Most people don't know this, but a grenade has a longer delay than the movies show you. Now, don't get me wrong, that little sucker is racing to explode in five seconds. So, my advice is not to dally.

I look behind me as I hear the grenade go off just in time to see a couple of mercs get caught in the truck's explosion. This then hits the gas tank, and the next thing you know, the truck fully explodes again. It rises like a fiery rocket, flipping over before crashing into the blackening snow and hissing like a dying dragon. When the explosion happens, I hit the ground and rise with a final salute.

"Fuck you!"

I fire half a mag in the enemy's general direction and then I'm off. Crashing through the woods, followed by bullets and curses, I link up with Reaper and Doc. They fall in behind me, and we crash off into the brush. I change magazines as we move forward. It's treacherous out here as we scramble over the rocks and snow, jumping over logs and small streams that have iced over from the frigid winter. It's really coming down, the snow covering our tracks, and it's the only thing saving our lives at this point. Doc yells into the wind through our comms.

"If we don't change this situation, we are severely screwed."

Reaper is in the lead when she suddenly veers to the right, calling for us to hurry. Luckily for us, she found a cabin, and we just might make it out of this alive.

It's times like this that I sometimes question my life choices, but I still wouldn't change a thing. They talk about convicts becoming institutionalized or programmed after so long in incarceration, and the same is true for anyone who works for the man, hanging it out there every day. No matter the job, when you wear your life on your sleeve in service of something higher, it changes you.

And there is no going back.

We hit the porch and look into the darkened interior through the front windows, then mule kick the door open and are inside in a matter of seconds. We know what's coming and what we have to do. They are both pros and in the face of overpowering odds, they never waiver. Reaper upends the kitchen table, and then she and I prop it against the front window, increasing our concealment. A bullet will still easily go through a normal table, easy peasy. Doc is laying out items, getting ready for the fight. He goes to the fireplace and quickly makes a fire with the already prepared wood stack.

As it takes hold of the dry wood, he places a fire poker inside to get hot.

If we have to go down, we're not going to make it easy for them. We're going Old West on these motherfuckers, and I mentally prepare to fight through searing pain if I get hit. Doc's and my eyes meet, and we share a look of mutual respect and understanding. I then slap Reaper on the shoulder as I pass the window where she's set up. I guard the door and act as a floater to cover the back. Doc posts up on the rear of the room, covering the side, and we get our heads in the game. I remember that I have a mouth guard and put it in now. It's a trick I picked up from an old ranger and it's saved my teeth more than once. I rotate my neck and loosen up my body as much as I can, willing the fight to start.

They don't disappoint, and the shooting begins moments later. Reaper returns fire, and the bullets really start to fly. The house is being shredded as lead swarms in from the mercs like angry bees. Pictures leap from the wall, and vases shatter as the deadly confetti rains down from the attacking aggressors.

I dodge through the wood splinters to shoot through the front door as I see a darkened shadow appear underneath it. Bullets pass in both directions, and I'm struck in the leg. It goes straight through the meat, and the pain sears its way along with it. Taking my breath away, I fall backward, still firing until my mag runs out. Doc's pulling me away towards the fireplace as I reload and continue laying down fire.

Fuck these guys!

Doc cuts my pants around the bullet hole, exposing the wound. Blood oozes from it, but not squirting, and that is a good sign: no artery nick. He grabs the glowing poker from the fire and looks at me. I steady myself, spitting out my mouth guard and biting down on the edge of my vest's shoulder strap. The pain is immediate as Doc taps the edges of the wound, searing the skin and closing the hole. I scream into the bite, and I fight hard not to pass out. The smell of my burned flesh, cordite, and Reaper's constant trash-talking keeps me in the game. I flip over, and Doc sears the other side as I ready my weapon, put in my mouth-guard, and I'm back in the fight.

As I get up from the floor, the front door explodes, and I catch a guy in the doorframe rushing in. He has a wicked shotgun but only gets the chance to drop it as I welcome him in with a batch of hot lead. As the battle rages around me, if I could stop and internally process, I would see that I've never felt more alive than in these moments of chaotic turmoil.

Death is dancing everywhere, and fate is like smoke drifting about. It's sheer will that makes someone not want to run and hide. This is not a sane act, and I'm reminded again of my neurodivergence as I smile and reload. I'm looking for a spot to get in the fight when I hear Reaper cry out as she takes a round in her upper shoulder.

As Doc drags her away from the window, I crawl up to take over her shooting position. I pop up, scan, shoot, then drop down and listen. I'm about to fire again when I hear Reaper cry out as Doc sears her wound shut.

It's at this moment when a stray bullet nicks the gas line, and the kitchen bursts into flames. We know the cabin is now on fire, but we keep fighting anyway. We are not running out just to be shot up. These guys had no idea about the shit storm they kicked up. When you are crazier than the situation, you have an immediate advantage.

And we are all seriously fucking nuts!

I'm up shooting again, laying down suppressive fire, when my rifle jams, and I have to dive back into cover. I quickly eject the mag, clear the jammed round, and then reset my mag before slapping the forward assist. Whenever I feel that bolt slam forward, my focus draws in, and I become lethal—like a door has been opened.

I hear Doc yell that Reaper's down and turn to see him working on her. She passed out from the pain, and Doc quickly grabs his weapon and starts shooting from around the door. I notice the cabin is now quickly filling up with smoke. We're holding them off for now, but I feel like they are regrouping for something.

I look over at Doc, seeing the grim set on his features as he scans his section, coughing in the smoke. Then I suddenly hear him yell.

"Contact right side!"

He moves outside the cabin and starts shooting around the corner. I join him as he falls back to reload, taking his firing position and keeping the heat on. They are flanking us, and it's a smart move. There are no firing positions along this side of the cabin, effectively creating a blind spot. I hear Reaper back in the fight and as she moves to the rear of the cabin closest to the fire, heading off their flanking attack. We would need to expose ourselves fully in order to effectively engage the enemy.

That's right, I said it...enemy.

The fight continues, and the longer it lasts, the more personal it becomes. Mercs lay bleeding, moaning, crying, and dying or already dead, littering the snow around the cabin. A quick scan tells me there was another group somewhere because there are a lot of bodies, and there is still more pressing the attack. They shout curses and taunts at us, clearly enraged that we would have the audacity to stand up against them.

Yeah, I have the audacity to do a lot of crazy shit.

Yelling out cover to Reaper, she immediately starts laying down fire, keeping them at bay. The flames behind her are escaping through the windows, setting the roof on fire.

I grab my other grenade and pull the pin, clenching it in my fist. Heading out the door, I stay as low as I can get. Adrenaline carries me past the pain of my bullet wound. I hook around the corner and throw the grenade baseball-style into the tree line; the spoon flying off as I release it. The effort of the throw hurtles me into a patch of slush.

The live grenade arcs through the air, then bounces off a huge pine and into the tree line before exploding a second later. Snow and forest debris explode from the edge of the clearing through the blizzard, and I begin to hear screaming. I low crawl back around the corner, my new injury burning in my thigh as I use the muscle. I'm surprised I'm not killed, and I take a minute when I'm back in the cabin to regain composure.

Doc has been firing from the door, and he yells over his shoulder, coughing into the smoke as he shoots.

"The tree line has caught fire!"

Smoke drifts through the storm, and visibility is dropping. It's now completely dark, and the fire is lighting up the area through the haze, strobing the night.

Doc suddenly takes one in the vest, and it knocks him down and away from the door. As he's catching his breath, I advance forward to stand over him, protecting him as I lay down deadly suppressive fire. My rifle roars as the smoking shell casings rain down around him—my life to protect his as the fire catches along the ceiling, spreading faster.

This is love.

He rises through the pain, slapping my shoulder. We switch places as he takes on the fight again, and I reload another magazine. I'm getting ready to switch with him again when I feel him jerk into me before falling. He has shielded me from the rounds that tore through his body. I drag him away from the door, but I can tell he's already gone from his eyes. I pull off his tags, shoving them in my pocket next to Johnson's. It's confusing to feel both the ache of a loss and to be thankful it was quick at the same time.

"Doc's gone!"

I see Reaper look back over her shoulder sadly before continuing the fight, screaming rage into the violent night.

"Motherfuckers!"

I punch the deteriorating wall before shouldering my weapon and advancing outside like an avenging angel, rifle blazing. I hit three before I'm dry and duck back inside to reload again.

RIP my brother.

I slap a fresh one in my weapon and notice it's my last mag. I need to conserve shots if I can. I will make each one count. I call out to Reaper.

"Last mag!"

Reaper yells back as she tosses me a full one.

"Here!"

She's struggling with the smoke and the encroaching fire, hunching away from it as she fights. I know it must be hot.

The magazine she threw is rotating through the smoldering air, almost as if in slow motion when I hear a muffled crump followed by a rumble from outside.

Someone has set off explosives at the high load point of the snow, right on the peak above us. The explosion breaks the bond, holding the massive sheets of ice in place. They start sliding downhill, gaining both speed and mass as tons of snow begin to hurtle down the mountain toward us with a growing rumble.

Reaper screams over the impending roar. It's the first time I have heard her sound afraid.

"Avalanche!"

I see the mercs begin to break contact, but I can tell they don't have enough time. I turn and run back into the cabin's interior, jumping over Doc's body, heading towards the fire as the rumble intensifies. I suddenly see the snow explode through the back door and wall, sweeping Reaper up into the deadly maelstrom of frozen death.

Then I'm spinning around, violently shaken, and carried in the snow. It has burning pieces of wood and debris every-where within it, and I collide with a burning timber while fighting to catch my breath. The last thing I see before I'm knocked out is a swirling, confusing dance of snow, fire, and blood.

Chapter Twenty-Seven

After they get picked up, the girls arrive in the area around thirty minutes later and circle the block while they figure out what to do next. They've heard about the Fowler Mansion and see the same car from the kidnapping parked in the driveway. After some back-and-forth, they decide on the direct approach. Svetlana and Aria will go to the front door and see what happens, while Nora will park as close as possible to the front door of the house and be on standby.

Nora parks then, with Alley leading the way, Aria and Svetlana walk nervously up to the front door. A smashed watermelon is in the driveway, and they look at each other, wondering how it got there. When they reach the door, they look at each other questioningly before Svetlana impulsively pushes the Ring doorbell. She hovers her finger close to the bell, blocking the camera. After a moment, an Asian man comes to answer. He's middle-aged and wears a driver's cap, which he readjusts as he sees the pretty girls standing there.

"How may I help you, miss?"

Aria takes the lead and responds directly, wondering what else to do. This day has been one for the books, so why stop now?

"We're here to pick up our friend...you know, the one you took earlier today; I'd like him back."

The man steps back, clearly surprised. Recovering, he awkwardly responds.

"Why don't you come in, and we can figure this whole thing out?"

Aria gives him an *"Are you crazy look?"* and he tries a different approach.

"Oh, I see he didn't tell you. We're old friends. I know it's ridiculous, but we have a wild sense of humor. Oh, the trouble we used to get into. Why don't you come inside, and he can explain all this when he..."

He thinks for a minute, clearly both a lousy liar and not the sharpest tool in the shed.

"He gets out of the bathroom. Stomach stuff, you know?"

He smiles at his oh-so-cheeky lie, oblivious to his complete transparency. Aria, clearly having figured out this guy is neither the boss nor very helpful, continues by being blunt.

"Can you go get your manager, crime boss, or whatever weasel is in charge of this sinking ship?"

This enrages the man, who rushes forward to grab Aria before sliding to a stop. He sees Svetlana filming him with her phone, smiling and waving. He stops like a deer in headlights as she speaks.

"I'm an influencer, you sack of shit. Say hello to my two point-five million followers. Oh, and I'm streaming live for all of them to see you...say cheese!"

Alley growls at him to make sure he gets the point. She lifts her nose and starts sniffing the air.

Aria shoots Svetlana an "Are you serious?" look that Svetlana just winks at, as the man covers his face.

Who is this chick?

The man then surprises everyone as he runs from the house, his hat flying off as he bolts away. While leaving, they hear him yelling.

"Fuck this, I did not sign up for this! Two thousand dollars, no way! I'm just a driver and don't want any of this shit to be pinned on me. I'm out of here."

Nora humorously watches this unfold from her spot next to the house and then calls Alley back over to her. This is partly to keep the dog safe but also to be ready when needed. She can feel the fight approaching in the wind like an evil tide, and she always likes to be aware of impending danger and stay ahead of the curve. Alley trots to the side of the car happily and sits obediently, still alert to the situation. She sniffs the grass and the ground and catches a familiar scent in the air.

Alpha.

Chapter Twenty-Eight

Hearing a commotion from upstairs, Boogie Nights and the grieving Mrs. Carpenter exchange glances before she looks at me. I'm looking around through my good eye, still trying to figure a way out of this mess.

"I'll see what's going on upstairs. Jerry is supposed to be up there, but I swear he's as useless as tits on a boar."

Boogie nods at the sage wisdom, clearly too thick to understand. As she leaves, Boogie looks at me and a smile creeps over his face. He walks over to me, and instead of punching me, he lightly rubs his finger up and down my chest suggestively. He smiles clearly, impressed with his range, as he whispers in my ear.

"Big tough guy like you. This has to make you uncomfortable, huh?"

He brings his face in front of mine, close yet outside of head-butting range. He has his hands on my thighs and massages them as he continues.

"Since it will be your first time, I'll make sure I'm extra rough. I don't want you to forget it in the little time you have left."

He smiles at me cruelly until I smile back, raising an eyebrow as I reply.

"What makes you think this is my first time? This is nothing...Come here, and I'll tell you a dirty little secret."

Boogie, caught up in the fantasy, eagerly leans closer to hear the juicy tea I'm about to spill.

When he's close enough, I bite around his ear as hard as possible. He lifts me off the ground as I hold on, my teeth firmly cutting into the flesh around his ear. He screams, hitting my head and trying to get me off of him. Finally, as he pulls me away, his ear comes with me.

He shrieks with his hand pressed firmly on his gaping wound. I see pure rage in his eyes as he comes in to make me pay. When he's almost on me, I spit his ear at him, hitting him in the forehead, momentarily breaking his concentration with the realization of what had just happened.

Hopping up on my feet awkwardly, I spin my chair around just as he collides with me. The force of the collision sends us both to the ground, and I feel the satisfying crunch as my chair breaks. I squirm out from under him, and we both struggle on the ground, trying to get to our feet. My left arm is still attached to the chair piece, and as all the other pieces of wood and debris fall away, I rise like a phoenix.

I'm reborn in this basement of pain and grief, and the sentiment seems appropriate.

My balance is off, and I sway as I stare down at this piece of shit. Fuck this guy...you want to fuck around with me? I guess you are about to find out what happens. He lunges toward me and hits the hanging light, which explodes this time and sends the room into sudden darkness.

I quickly dodge to the side, sending him flying with a flick of my wrist. He supplied all the power, sending him violently into the shelving with a crunch. As he rises, I hear a grandfather clock somewhere chime, announcing a change in time. I'm getting woozy from all the exertion and blood loss, when suddenly my world goes black.

Chapter Twenty-Nine

It happened so fast.

As Svetlana and Aria enter the house, a woman comes around the corner, startled by their appearance. Aria can tell the woman's been crying and feels a weird camaraderie with her pain. She looks like shit, and mascara runs down her face like yesterday's news. Jenny recovers quickly and then makes her demands.

"Who are you? What are you doing inside my house? Jerry!"

Aria looks Jenny directly in the eye, all empathy lost.

"He knew what was best for him and ran away. Where's our friend, bitch?"

Aria's fists come up, ready to fight Jenny, who quickly realizes the situation has spiraled wildly out of control, like a spinning top dancing along the edge of a chasm.

Texas hears the commotion in the hallway, but the bedazzled bonehead doesn't offer any help. She's perched on a chair, wiping her face with a waitress uniform, still crying her squinty little eyes out from her confrontation with Guy earlier.

Hearing Janse's scream, Jenny runs for the stairs, yelling to Texas.

"Don't let them leave!"

A grandfather clock in the hallway begins to chime.

Everything is spinning out of control! Jenny wanted a long, painful punishment for the one and only Guy Castle, but this was getting ridiculous!

Janse lied to Jenny about being in the special operations community and wanting to help her. She knew he worked for her aunt, but seriously? That guy is a psycho, and her radar has been pinging on him since they met. He doesn't look the type with that cheesy mustache. She finishes that thought when she gets to the bottom of the stairs and opens the door.

As the light from the hallway illuminates the dark room, Jenny sees Janse is bent over an unconscious Guy. As she takes more in, he startles and turns toward her. She notices he has Guy's pants pulled down.

What the hell?

"Uh...I can explain. This is not what..."

She suddenly can't hear anything else besides an ear-splitting scream, and it takes her fracturing mind a second to recognize it as her own. Jenny runs back up the stairs as Janse follows a moment later while struggling to pull up his pants.

Hearing the commotion from outside, Nora grabs her purse and exits the vehicle. This has gone on long enough, and she will go in there and do the same thing she does with wild animals.

Assert Dominance.

Alley whines next to her, and she looks down reproach-fully, reminding the animal who is in charge. When the screaming starts, it's all too much for Alley, and she begins to run for the front door.

"Alley!"

Following the scent inside, Alley almost knocks over a human as they meet on the stairs. She let him go, as she has more significant priorities, but she recognizes his scent from earlier. She makes it to the bottom of the steps in three bounds and leaps into the door, knocking it open.

Alpha!

She runs to her master and excitedly licks his face. As she continues to do this, Guy regains consciousness. He momentarily picks the fight back up before Alley lies on his dirty and abused chest, calming him. The warm fur and reassuring weight bring Guy back, and he loses it for a moment.

Guy tears up, taken by the emotional rollercoaster his life is on right now. As he silently cries, his head buried in Alley's soft fur, she leans into him as if to hug him and tell him it's going to be okay.

This just makes him cry harder.

When Aria and Svetlana are left with Texas, it's obvious that she's way outclassed. They glare at each other a moment before Texas wilts under the gaze and pretends to inspect her rhinestone sequins adorning the front of her cowgirl getup. They are all startled when they hear Jenny scream and then run up the stairs, sobbing.

What the hell happened?

Svetlana finds this whole thing funny—the drama people create to fill their time. She has been recording the entire thing on her phone, and she's enjoying making Texas squirm under her judgment-filled gaze.

They are all shocked once again as Jenny comes sobbing back into the room a moment later, being chased by a bleeding man who looks a lot like...

OMG, Janse!

Svetlana is startled to recognize him. This is all too much for Aria, who races to the stairs, after passing the newest contestants on; the Drama is Rife.

Looking through tear-blurred eyes, Jenny notices something. Janse quit trying to explain himself the moment he saw Oleg's wife, Svetlana.

How do they know each other?

While this is happening, Aria gets to the bottom of the stairs, seeing Alley lying on a pile of bloody rags.

As she gets closer, she realizes Alley is protecting a crying Guy, and the sight of him broken and bloody, his battered body lying on a pile of debris as he sobs into her fur, is seared in Aria's mind forever. She has never seen Guy like this before. She rushes to his side and drops to grab one of his hands. Alley glances at her before scanning the room, protecting her Guy.

Upstairs, a stern Mrs. James stomps into the house, and she yells with authority to grab everyone's attention.

"That is enough!"

The small front room is in chaos as unique personalities and agendas clash. Things click for Jenny, suddenly. Her eyes get prominent as she cocks her head and looks from Janse to Texas and then Svetlana.

What is the one thing they all have in common?

The crypto-locker!

Mrs. James is trying to take control of the situation, but is finding it difficult. The only one she has kowtowed to is Texas, which is not saying too much. The room falls silent when Aria appears supporting a beaten and bloody Guy.

Janse, aka Boogie Nights, moves toward Aria threateningly, and Alley appears from behind her. Her head is lowered, and she growls as she moves in front of Aria toward a bleeding one-eared-maggot, baring her teeth. Janse grins a cruel grin and brings up a pistol no one knew he had.

A single gunshot breaks the tension and silence of the room. Everyone looks at Janse to see a small smoking hole in his shirt, which begins to stain with blood...a lot of blood. As Janse falls for the last time with shock written across his face, everyone turns and looks at a calm and composed Nora James. She's holding a little pink number, smoke rising from the barrel.

Jenny begins to scream as all this madness unfolding in her new mansion becomes too much. Alley and company then leave while a calm Nora holds Jenny and Texas at gunpoint.

"Now don't let this whole ordeal affect your patronage at The Paw Spa, we truly love Bunny."

She says this as Aria is dragging Guy out the door when he stops her with his hand on the doorjamb. He turns painfully to Jenny and speaks.

"You know we're not done yet, but you're Doc's widow, and it's not going to end like this. Get a pen and paper, I can help you with this mess...I'll wait here."

He says this last part sarcastically, and Jenny grabs a pen and a piece of mail on the table next to her. Guy then gives her a phone number before giving instructions.

"Tell them you are calling about the Sanguinus gala, and you need a caterer and a cleaning party immediately. Tell them your Uncle Tanner is paying for it, and his card is on file. If they ask about the weather, say it's stormy. Do this now, and a cleaning and disposal team will be here to clean up this mess and get rid of the body within the hour."

Guy stops for a second and then debates with himself before looking at Jenny. Their eyes meet, and the pain they share is clear in their features.

"Doc was an excellent operator, Mrs. Carpenter, and he was a friend. He was a great man, and I miss him every day, just as you do."

With that final thought, Aria lugs Guy outside and into Nora's car. Guy passes out again as he's being loaded in, but not before saying,

"Hey! Nice car..."

Chapter Thirty

The hot water drips slowly as it ripples the surface, causing the roll of a hollow echo to blend in with the steamy air. Thick drops of red stain the water, melding together as they swirl, creating a temporary art form. It's a fading vision that is both similar and unique to the pain that slowly caused its transition. A white washcloth plunges into the darkening water with a splash, absorbing the color like a sponge before it's brought up and touching the battered body of Guy Castle.

Dancing in a hurricane while trying to stay in the eye, he spins increasingly out of control. When the luminescence of what appears to be angels blinds him, he pauses. They lower their hands down into the icy water of his mortality, then pull him painfully up to the surface once again. The angels have cleansed his wounds and protected him many times before, and this day is no different. As the small wet towel pats his burning skin, it soothes him and slowly brings him back. Struggling to open his eyes, he hears a faint whisper as they disappear.

"Good luck, Guy."

My eyelids feel like they are glued shut, but eventually they open. My vision is impaired, blurry, and my perception is like a camera trying to find focus. As I fight every part of my sluggish body, I look around the room and realize I'm back at the hotel. I wonder if any other drama in the past has unfolded here in this suite, and then I quickly decide I don't want to know.

How did I get here?

It feels like flames are touching my skin, and it's on fire, but it seems pretty familiar and warranted. My dreams were a jumbled madness of screaming voices, terrible violence, and screeching tires. I try to clear the memories of those fever dreams and sit up.

Where are my tags?

My hand searches against my chest in a panic for the dog tags until Svetlana assures me as she touches my arm gently.

"Don't worry, Guy. Your necklace is right there on the night-stand next to you."

I reach for it like it's air, like I'm underwater, struggling to come up. Instantly I feel the anxiety depart slipping them on, as their light but a heavy presence is back against my body.

I guess I need my ghosts as much as they need me.

As their whispering judgment falls back into the low-level noise of my life, I remember what has happened to me. I turn my body slightly, cringing at the pain as Svetlana tuts and worries over me like a concerned nurse. It cracks me up. I wonder if she even has any type of medical training. I'm examining the state my body is in. I know for sure that my nose has been broken and reset since I'm breathing through the painful, ragged tunnel, and I'm pretty sure I have a cracked rib.

A soft sobbing sound coming from the other room inter-rupts my self-examination. Svetlana and I exchange a glance before I flick my chin towards the door. She smiles and nods, getting up from the side of the bed and returns the washcloth to the water. As she walks away, I enjoy the sight of her leaving, and it shows me I'm not as hurt after all.

I've healed from worse and will come back from this.

I reassure myself that everything will be okay. But I also secretly acknowledge the fact that I'm scared these wounds will never heal, and I'll be in pain forever. I know it's just my brain taking me on a wild ride, but that still doesn't quiet the mean little voice. I hear another soft sound, a dog whining.

"Woof!"

Alley raises her head, and I see her guarding me on the floor beside my bed. I lower my arm over the edge, barely brushing her fur with my fingers. She eagerly rises into my hand, leaning against the bed, and gives me a dog hug. I ruffle her fur and pet her soft, thick ears. She's magnificent, and I can't believe how lucky I am that we found each other.

"Hey girl, I missed you. Did you miss me?"

At this, I get another bark and wonder what she thinks I'm saying. Looking into her brown eyes, I see concern and judgment, and I believe she's telling me not to do anything stupid again. I laugh at this as I remind myself that we have just met and still have a lot to learn about each other. I'm glad she's okay, which makes me remember the bigger picture. It's coming at me like waves: the Patinko house ambush, the Svetlana chase and killing that assassin, Aria being kidnapped, and...

Oh, my God...Avery!

My heart breaks all over again. My emotions are raw, and my eyes blur with tears. I turn my head to the side so no one will see me crying, and I try to let it out slowly. As the tears roll down my face, they cascade off the side of my newly set nose. I'm in so much pain right now, both internally and externally. I don't even give a shit that I was kidnapped; the way I see it, I was chauffeured to my destiny, care of a grieving widow. I failed her like I failed Doc. I failed them all.

I wish these ghosts would drag me under. I want to give up.

Then, in my medicated-induced, hallucinating mind, I see Johnson come in, smiling at me as he enters. Reaper follows him in, flipping me off as she grins and chin nods me. Doc follows right behind with a concerned look on his face. I was surprised when Avery was following right behind them and looking upset. They have all surrounded my bed and are looking down at me. I feel subconscious and almost sit up before Doc puts a reassuring hand on my chest, lightly pressing me back down on the bed.

What the hell?

I look around at each of my constant companions and wonder if Avery has now joined the crew. Of course she has, I laugh to myself. My eyes land on Reaper, who smiles lethally at me. Her smile is so cold it would make a ghost shudder.

"Stop being a pussy."

Well, okay, I guess that's her bedside manner. Good thing she's not a doctor. I think that, as she bends down towards me, getting in my face. A part of her brown hair falls from behind her ear, and it feels like a curtain is hiding us.

"What? This is the new you. Some badass you turned out to be. What the fuck, man! Why are you acting this way...like you're giving up?"

She spits this last part out like poison, and I feel her disdain. When I look over at Avery, I feel embarrassed for some reason. It's like she's silently judging me, and I think I see her nod in agreement.

I would never give up on you.

"Bud, if you give up on yourself, you kind of give up on all of us."

My head turns to the smiling Johnson, and he nods sadly. As he continues, he opens his arms wider with his palms up.

"Ops go bad, man...shit happens. We knew the risk, which was part of the rush. You take on too much responsibility for what happened. You know, you spin the wheel enough times; eventually, it will land on your number."

I want to argue with him, tell him I underestimated the Sparrow, and it was my fault, but all I can do is mumble out a few words.

"Because of me, we lost three good operators that day."

Doc gets my attention with a barking laugh before turning serious.

"That was not on you, bro. That was on the Sparrow. And we lost four good operators because of this, not three. You need to let it go, man."

I can't.

"That's always been your problem, you know?"

This is from Avery. I look at her with questioning eyes.

"You never let things go if YOU DECIDE, but have no problem letting go of anything you deem not mission critical."

She says the last part with finger air quotes, and the statement slaps me hard across my now bruised ego.

She's right.

"You want to know what my problem with you has always been? You will drag anyone into your problems if it helps you out, but you never think about what that will cost the other person. I'm dead because of someone else's issues. Because of you, my story was cut short."

Avery's words slice through me like a scalpel, and I know I will have these fresh scars forever. She's right. I say something silently, but I can't respond. As in life, my team still has my back. Unsurprisingly, it's Reaper who comes to my defense first.

"Hold on, Guy didn't choose for any of this to happen. You rushed in there alone and like a chicken with her head cut off...didn't you?"

"I had to save my sister, bitch! There were just too many of them. I had no chance...and this one guy..."

Avery trails off, putting her hand up and covering her eye as she remembers the trauma. Johnson, beside her, puts his arm around her shoulders reassuringly. Reaper changes focus from Avery and turns her attention to me, her hair again falling, only this time it brushes my cheek. The wind picks up, and I notice flurries falling. The weather gets increasingly intense as my ghosts stare down at me with their clothes flapping in the building gale. Reaper bends down to talk into my ear. The snowstorm has picked up.

"We all made our own choices...Guy?"

She snaps her fingers, getting my attention, and looks at me intensely. I notice the flicker of fire reflecting in her retinas as she yells into the blizzard.

"Remember who you are!"

Chapter Thirty-One

Aria sits at the hotel desk, staring at a dark computer screen she's not seeing. Her focus is a thousand miles away. Her mind is awash in shades of grief, confusion, and loss, and she feels truly alone for the first time, and it terrifies her. People around her glide through their lives, using their talents and living their dreams.

How am I going to live now?

The bleak thought brings on another sob, and Aria puts her head on the desk. She presses her forehead into the surface and feels the tears falling like rain. Her brain usually has the answers she needs, and she's become used to it. The last few days have been one big blur, and the little sleep she has gotten since her life changed has been short and fitful. Aria is full of a cold emptiness she could never have imagined.

Avery, I miss you.

She has never experienced this before and now realizes this new emotion is what she will feel whenever she imagines her sister... her twin... her best friend... her other half. What is she going to do? Her world has been turned upside down, and she doesn't know the new rules. She knows her sister wanted to be cremated, and the thought of that brings on a fresh wave of pain.

I can't do this.

Aria is still crying, and Svetlana comes up from behind and consolingly places a hand on her shoulder. She has known plenty of anguish but can tell this is different, more intimate...closer. Aria's heartbreak radiates off her like heat, and when Svetlana rubs her back, Aria shudders, bringing on a heavy flow of sorrow and misery.

Svetlana thinks this is too much as she empathizes with a grieving Aria. Guilt bears heavily upon her as she wonders what part she played in this nightmare. She knows she's not innocent and has some blame. Money has always been the source of comfort and displeasure in her life, and it seems like it's still a constant. She indeed conspired with the psychopathic mustache man, planning to use him to do her "heavy lifting" to acquire the crypto-locker from Oleg, but she had no idea how crazy he was. She also didn't know about his connection to the widow, Jenny.

Svetlana is tired of being used, feeling lonely, and only having personal relationships when they can benefit her somehow. If she digs deep, she knows it's because of her childhood and the hard lessons she learned growing up. She craves a connection but is too scared to let down her guard, as it always ends up burning her.

Trust?

What is trust?

We give it to people freely yet are stung deeply when it's abused. If we know we are fallible creatures, why do we still fall for the same old traps? The pain we feel when deceived is the same pain our ancestors felt millions of years ago, yet we have never evolved past this.

Why?

But am I any better? I have used people just as much as I have been used, maybe more. I feel pain when I discover I have been lied to, yet I will turn around and lie. Why is that different?

As she thinks these thoughts, she comforts Aria. Her guilt bothers her, and she could never have expected to develop a friendship through shared adversity, yet that happened.

Aria needed her help and asked. There were no games or negotiations; she saw Svetlana's value and asked for help. It was so simple yet deeply profound to her, as she didn't come from that place, that honest world. It feels like a pure light shining into a dark, dusty room. The beam breaks through the swirling dust motes and darkness, illuminating everything equally within its gaze.

Aria might be the first genuine person I have met, and I secretly hurt her.

As she continues to console a grieving Aria, Svetlana's guilt threatens to consume her whole. Standing behind Aria like this, comforting her, she's too close to it all. She feels like she's jumping out of her skin as the feeling refuses to go away. As much as it seems against her character, she needs to come clean to expel this toxic acid that she has been holding inside.

"Aria, I'm so sorry! This is all my fault!"

With this, she joins in with a crying Aria, and they both are stuck in this moment before Aria responds with shuddered breaths.

"You...you didn't cause this. What are you talking about?"

Aria looks behind her, and Svetlana sees just how glossy and red her eyes are. She has seen this pain before; she just can't remember where it came from. It feels good to get this weight off her chest, and she continues talking faster and faster.

"Oleg...I overheard Oleg talking one night about the business and how the funds would be merged for an impending power grab by her niece, Jenny Fowler. The accounts would be used for leverage to take over Harriet Fowler's operations, and if they are not acquired, then cashed out. I saw this as an opportunity to get away from someone else's shadow and start my life over again for me."

She shifts uncomfortably before continuing, absently scratching an imaginary itch on the side of her thigh.

"I panicked when I heard Jenny was bringing in her cousin to help, so I contacted Janse through a third party, planning to use him to get the crypto-locker and then have him take any legal blowback, insulating myself from any crimes being committed. He worked for Harriet and would have been perfect...how you say... patsy."

With this last statement, she hangs her head in shame. A tear runs down her cheek and along her sculpted lip before traveling down to drip off her chin, forgotten forever. Aria sits there, absorbing it in. After a moment and a few sniffs, Svetlana continues.

"This spun so out of control, and then when I was ambushed and my house destroyed, then pursued by mysterious assassins, I knew it was out of my control completely and panicked... I played dumb and wanted to see how it would play out... I'm so sorry!"

Aria turns around in her chair toward Svetlana and grabs her hand. With an intensity only born through incredible pain and with tears streaming from her eyes, her scratchy voice honestly responds.

"Svet, I don't blame you for trying to improve your life. I see why you did what you did. You are not the one responsible for my sister's death; someone else is, and I'm going to find her. I heard my kidnappers talking about her, about someone named Texas."

I'm coming for you, Birdy.

This thought hits Aria in two diverse ways. One aspect of her is like a raging fire that wants to violently burn all those responsible, while the other part is sad and feels the loss of her humanity in the willingness to be consumed by that fire. She knows this will change her forever, but then she reminds her altruistic self that she's already a changed person. She lost her other half...

Nothing is worse than that.

***

Svetlana brings Aria's thoughts back as she hugs her, sitting in the chair, and thanks her repeatedly for her kindness and forgiveness. She holds on for a long time, and both women comfort each other in that moment, a genuine friendship born.

When the moment has passed, Svetlana takes control, seeing the distraught Aria is too far in grief to think rationally.

"Aria, I know this is hard, but did Avery ever tell you what she wanted done when she..."

She stops awkwardly, wringing her hands, unsure of how to gently put it. Aria looks up at Svetlana, lost for a moment, before slowly nodding her head.

"Cremated. We both wanted to be cremated, but I don't know how...what to..."

With this, Aria breaks down again, and Svetlana comforts her new friend as best she can.

"You not worry. I call the hospital for you and take care of everything. You are not alone, Sestryonka."

It shocks Svetlana that she called Aria Sestryonka, or little sister, but it seems appropriate in some way, and she decides she likes it. Arranging everything with the hospital takes her around ten minutes. Aria stares blankly at the wall the whole time, lost in her sad thoughts.

After finishing with the hospital, the girls are quietly talking when they hear moans coming from the bedroom—and not the good kind. When they enter the room, they see Guy squirming around in bed, sleeping, talking to someone. His blankets are twisted, and his T-shirt is soaked with sweat. As they approach the bed, it sounds to Svetlana like he's pleading with someone.

I don't want to know what's going on in your tortured mind.

As Guy deliriously tries to get out of bed, Svetlana places a hand on his chest, gently pushing him back down. She's slightly alarmed at how hot his skin is to the touch and makes a mental note to get some antibiotics. She then has a thought of which she's not too proud.

If he dies, he takes the knowledge of where the crypto-locker is to his grave.

She looks back at Guy and sees that Aria is standing beside him, holding Guy's hand. Alley is at the foot of the bed, and in such a large place, they are huddled next to each other. Svetlana notices this and wonders at its significance, wishing she were smart enough to see the pattern, not realizing she just had.

I guess we are all in this together now.

Chapter Thirty-Two

Banging around like loose change in a metal trash can, the next few days are a jumbled mess of loud emotions, shared sorrow, and fever dreams. Svetlana found medicine for Guy, and they decide to lay low for a few days in the suite, to let the storm pass. They rent a second room so they can spread out more. Guy's no good to anyone, lost in his medicated cocoon of suffering, hallucinations and healing.

Alley, his constant companion and now guard, refuses to leave his side except for once in the morning and once at night to do her business. Aria and Svetlana have taken turns walking next to Alley when she goes downstairs, as she still refuses to wear a leash, and both have marveled at how smart and in tune with everything she seems. Plus, with everything that has happened lately, it's nice to count on her security. She has shown what she's capable of, but only Alley knows that is only a glimpse of her true potential.

After a week, the hotel decides the group needs to move out and pushes the eject button. They find themselves outside the building after settling the hefty bill. It's incredible how you can be kicked out of a place while they still express how glad they are you stayed with them. Svetlana was happy to see the crypto-locker when Guy mumbles the safe code to her and volunteers to hold on to it "for safekeeping."

They borrow a wheelchair from the hotel doctor, and with Guy slumped in it, doped to his gills, for the painful transport home, they head outside. Svetlana is looking around in her usual intense way as Aria stares off into space, her hand on the back of Guy's wheelchair. She's startled when, unexpectedly, Svetlana speaks.

"Where is this transport? We said 10am, right?"

She says this to no one and finishes by blowing a raspberry with her lips as she dismissively waves her hand. Aria had suggested they hire a medical transport company to get Guy home. Aria looks at her watch and sees it's just after ten and is about to respond when they both see an ambulance pulling into the hotel. It parks in front of them, and a man and a woman exit and walk toward them. The woman is heavyset and short, while her partner is tall and skinny—the perfect pair. If Guy were present and not blasted off into his own outer space, he would have a quip, but he can only manage to drool.

"I take it this is our patient here?"

This is from the woman as she smiles at Svetlana, clearly used to people being kind to her bad jokes. Unfortunately, Svetlana is not one of them. She stares at the grinning pumpkin until her smile falters, and she gets to work. They load Guy up without further social platitudes and leave the parking lot five minutes later.

As they pull out of the hotel and accelerate down the street, they don't see the dark vehicle pull out and get behind them. The worst tail is an active tail, and they are completely unaware that they have just grown one. The driver is good and stays about three car lengths behind, invisible to the clueless EMTs, following the ambulance like a hungry lawyer. When the medical transport ambulance arrives at Guy's walk down, the car parks about a block away, watching.

The EMTs help Guy inside and into his bed, all under the watchful eye of Svetlana, whom they both fear. As they are leaving, they pass a well-dressed Asian man standing in the doorway. He politely moves inside to allow the EMTs to pass, who thank him, unaware they were just his key to get inside.

Jiro Kawakami wears an expensive black suit and black gloves, one hand holding an expensive black cane. He has classic, strong Japanese features and smiles politely, but the smile doesn't extend to his eyes; it's more mechanical. Aria is sitting at Guy's table, when she is suddenly startled to see him standing in the front room.

"Can I help you?"

Aria inquires, more perplexed than alarmed at the sudden appearance of this well-dressed stranger in black. He doesn't respond immediately; instead, he scans the spaces around him as if looking for something. Alarm bells go off in Aria's mind, and she sees the situation change radically. She hopes he can't speak English, so she tries again, this time in Japanese, and asks him if he needs help.

"Kon'nichiwa, otetsudai dekimasu ka?"

Surprised, Jiro turns to her, clearly impressed. He walks over to her, taking five steps, then bows slightly, before replying in Japanese.

"Hello, young miss. I'm looking for something that I lost."

He waits a moment to see if Aria understands him. She tilts her head to the side and replies, again in Japanese, with a look of confusion.

"Well, sir, I'm confused. What makes you think you lost something here?"

This entire conversation is weird, and Aria is stalling for time. He's about to respond when a startled Svetlana emerges from Guy's room.

"Who the hell is this?"

She looks at him up and down, begrudgingly nodding at his impeccable style. When she sees the look on Aria's face, she intuitively knows why this man is standing before them. Her mind races as she casually walks over to her purse containing the crypto-locker.

"Oh Moy! I'm such a mess in front of such a handsome gentleman!"

She picks up her purse and walks back into the bedroom.

"I'll be right back; I want to freshen up."

She winks at him but knows it's a thin lie. She has no time for anything better, and she feels her anxiety spike through her body like a cold show. Jiro watches her with a slight smile, while Aria is rooted to the chair, acting casual. The ninja looks back at Aria before beginning to follow Svetlana into the bedroom.

Nora James, as always, has impeccable timing and calls from the top of the stairs, just as Alley is exiting the bedroom, curious about what is going on. When the dog sees the ninja, she bares her teeth and starts to low growl. He might have the others fooled, but Alley recognizes the danger. This startles the man in black, and when Nora enters from the stairs, he changes tactics. With a curt nod, he turns and leaves Guys' apartment, passing a perplexed Mrs. James along the way.

"Well, what was that about?"

She wonders aloud as she walks up to Alley. She ruffles Alley's fur and scratches her ears, all to Alley's pleasure. She went from on alert to panting happily in less than a minute.

Meanwhile, Svetlana is still in the room and in a state of panic. She has nowhere she can think of to stash the crypto-locker she currently has in her sweaty hand. She will have to hide it here, but doesn't want to be that obvious about it. She thinks about Guy's closet but worries it will be too obvious, so she walks back out, having heard Mrs. James. She casually sits on the couch, sliding the crypto-locker between the cushion and the end. She shifts to look at Nora.

"Who was that guy? He gave me the creeps!"

Svetlana looks at Aria, and they share a knowing look. It's better not to drag Nora into this mess.

"I have no clue, my dear. Was he a Jehovah's Witness?"

She looks at Aria as she floats this balloon, but it pops quickly.

"I don't think so...he only spoke Japanese."

Nora thinks the matter is pretty odd but turns her attention to Guy's room. Ironically, there are three women in his apartment, and he's completely incapacitated. She walks to the doorframe and leans in for a second, looking at Guy before straightening and sitting at the table next to Aria.

"Our poor Guy."

She says this, and it has become his collective name when they, unfortunately, must come together, all worried about his latest misadventure. It cracks Aria up, the way it sounds, and she lets out a small bark of a laugh.

Svetlana gets up from the couch and joins the women at the table. Nora is looking concerned at a zoned-out Aria, and Svetlana reassures her.

"She will be fine. She needs to go on this painful journey; the sooner she does, the quicker she will return to the light."

This response surprises Nora, who realizes she has been underestimating this beautiful young woman next to her. The poetry there speaks of deep knowledge and unfortu-nate experience. She's beginning to see Svetlana in a whole new way.

"With you as a friend, my dear, I have no doubt."

This genuine compliment makes Svetlana smile, and she nods in thanks. Her stomach growls suddenly, and she realizes she has eaten nothing since early that morning and that was out of a vending machine. Mrs. James hears it as well and smiles at the two young women.

"Come on, ladies...let's get some lunch. It's on me."

Svetlana nods her head, clearly liking the idea. She looks nervously over at the couch for a second before calming herself, knowing no one else knows where she put it.

Wasn't it supposed to be that if you hid something in plain sight, it would be harder to find?

She can't remember, but everyone is getting up, so she does, too. She will give Guy some more medicine if they'll be gone for a bit. She doesn't know what she's doing, but wants to do something. So, she rummages in her purse, pulling out an orange pill bottle. It says Dilaudid, which doesn't sound that strong to her.

She wonders what it has been diluted with, but realizes it doesn't matter.

She will give him two, just to be safe.

Chapter Thirty-Three

Jiro Kawakami of the Ban Clan returns to his car and formulates a plan. There were too many women in that tiny apartment, and things could have gotten messy, and he doesn't like to do messy things. As he walks, he replays what he observed back in his mind. A laughably easy lock, mail slot in the door, no cameras, or other alarm systems. One old smoke detector that he knew the brand of, so no hidden camera there. He could not see into the bedroom because of the dog, and that could be a problem. Luckily, he has creative ways of dealing with dogs nonlethally.

You never want to leave waves when moving in the smoke.

His grandfather used to say that to him, and it has stuck to this day. Plus, he likes dogs and respects their loyalty.

He arrives back at his car and gets in, giving his surroundings one last scan. Sitting there, he watches intently, and to his surprise, five minutes later, the three women exit and walk up the steps to the sidewalk. He watches them leave, wondering if this is some type of trap. The job is a simple theft, and the client specifically did not want Guy to be harmed. When he asked for more information, she simply told the truth.

"A favor given is a favor received."

Whatever, as long as he gets paid, he doesn't care. He uses his home-brewed scent blocker, carefully applying it to get an even coat. He then pulls some beef jerky from his glove box, takes out a nice big piece, and coats it with a powerful sleep oil he made himself. After returning his supplies to the glove box, he exits his vehicle and casually returns to Guy's apartment.

He takes his time, scanning and accessing his environment, looking for anything out of the ordinary. You have to be extra careful with the easy jobs as they are the ones you are more likely to mess up on, underestimating the situation and overestimating your abilities. It must always be balanced. Otherwise, chaos will reign, and the situation will spin out of control. He imagines holding water in one hand and fire in the other. He must juggle it constantly to keep from burning himself or splashing the water away.

As he finishes this thought, he arrives at the steps leading down to Guy's place. He listens intently for a few minutes before melting into the shadows at the bottom of the stairs in front of the door. He bends down and slides the beef jerky through the mail slot before banging hard on the door, just once.

He hopes the scent blocker will work and, a moment later, hears the dog sniffing curiously from the other side of the door. He then hears the sound he has been waiting for as the dog devours the jerky treat before retreating back into the other room. He hazards a peak through the mail slot, scanning the immediate area.

After a few moments of complete silence, he's sure the dog is now sleeping. He produces his picking tools as if by magic and opens the door within five seconds. He pushes it open silently before quietly entering, then shuts it carefully behind himself. He stands there momentarily, scanning the environment again, assessing possible hiding spots.

The fire department uses directional searches to not miss anything, and he decides to do that here. Choosing a *"left-hand search,"* he turns left, starts at the door, and searches everything stealthily, always moving left and following the wall. He knows what the crypto-locker looks like, which helps narrow down the possible hiding spots.

Continuing to use deduction and a left-hand search, Jiro finds the device a couple minutes later while searching under the couch cushions. He almost didn't check, as who would do that, but is glad that he did.

Amateurs.

On his way out, he peeks into the room, silently observing the sleeping pair. This guy will never know how lucky he was or that a real ninja was standing in his doorway. Few people live when a ninja's shadow falls against them...not many at all.

His ego wins out over common sense, and he impulsively carves the Japanese Kanji symbol for luck in his doorframe.

Let him figure that out.

He knows this is against his teachings and code, but the feeling also excites him, and he quickly leaves, not bothering to be quiet any longer. He locks the door behind him as the occupants sleep, smiling and thinking.

We wouldn't want him to get robbed!

Chapter Thirty-Four

The following week was all about the move for the two young women. Aria and Svetlana were inseparable the whole time, with Svetlana helping pack Avery's stuff after Aria took a few things to remember her dear twin by. Svetlana had nothing, as all her things were destroyed in the fire, so the girls had a few fun shopping days and tried to blow off the stress from the past two weeks.

In the last two weeks, Aria has settled into her pain. It's her new constant, and even though she and Guy have never spoken of it, they now have another thing in common...

Their ghosts.

Even in the darkest times, there can still be light, and Svetlana has become that flickering candle for Aria. Her constant companionship has helped more than she could ever explain. Since losing Avery, Aria has been terrified of being alone. It will feel like a final goodbye or an example of her new reality, and she can't take how loud that silence will become. Trapped in that echoing loneliness, she's worried she will spiral down until she's nothing....

Avery would be so ashamed of you!

The thought shocks Aria, and she internally reprimands herself for her slip-up within her self-imposed rule sets.

Must not show weakness.

Aria is debating with herself, lost in her thoughts, and she's startled when Svetlana enters her room to wave Guy's credit card.

"We should probably give this back at some point, but want to order pizza first?"

Despite herself, Aria smiles at this. Even after everything that has happened recently, Svetlana has such an easy nature about her.

How does she do it?

Aria's stomach growls, answering the question, and both women snicker at the irony. She hasn't been eating much lately, and pizza does sound good.

Meanwhile, Arias's stomach is growling, so is the current client in room number four. Nora James has had enough of this canine's hissy fit, save that for those horrible cats she's already decided. Composing herself, she talks calmly but sternly to her current furry fighting fury.

"That is enough, mister! SEBASTIAN, you know better than this! You will SIT down now!"

The dog's butt hits the tile, and he looks around, confused, not realizing she just plugged into his unconscious learned behavior. He looks back at Nora, tilting his head briefly before getting up.

"Oh NO, you don't, SEBASTIAN. You will SIT and STAY!"

Sebastian automatically sits down again.

"If you don't STAY, you will not get a TREAT."

At the mention of treat, the dog's tongue starts to drool and hang partially out of his mouth, and he pants happily. He tilts his head again, then lays down like it's his idea, and happily waits, observing the room. Nora, seeing this, nods her head once in a *"now it's final"* movement before exiting the room.

She passes the junior groomer who is about to walk in and says in an authoritative tone,

"Don't be afraid to take charge, dear. Remember that dogs like to know where they belong in the pack, so show them!"

With that final exclamation, Nora heads down the hall to room 1, the master primping and pampering suite. Nora designed it herself, and it's her favorite place at work. Thinking momentarily, she recalls Bunny is her next client. She loves that dog.

So well behaved and...the stories!

At first, she didn't believe the stories. I mean, a millionaire dog. But...

Crazier things have happened.

She pushes that thought out of her mind and smiles as she enters the room, calling to the happy miniature poodle.

"Bunny! You little stinker, you want a treat?"

She always gives the dogs a treat before she starts. It's better she begins with that than with a loud pair of clippers. She learned that lesson the hard way and still has a scar on her hand to remind her.

Bunny is wagging her little tail sitting on the raised central dais. She's so well-behaved. As Nora pets Bunny, she unclips her leash and, thinking about it, takes off her collar as well. She's going to get a bath, and her collar is expensive—that much is obvious.

The rich!

Even though she tries to emulate them, she will never get them, and she shakes her head with a chuckle. A dog collar with zirconia gems studded along its leather banding. She rubs the leather between her fingers, marveling at its softness and overall quality. As she looks closer, she can't help but notice the way the gems shine.

Oh my God, these are genuine diamonds!

Her fingers go numb as she holds something worth over a million dollars in her hand. Her mind is stunned that a person, no matter how rich, would buy something like this for their dog.

Where is there even a business that sells these?

She marvels at the collar, turning it over in her hands, and discovers a series of numbers and letters stamped into the back of the leather banding. She instantly recognizes this as a code.

But to what?

Chapter Thirty-Five

Guy is sitting on his couch and recuperating from his multiple injuries, but it's taking a while, and he's getting bored. He was never a good patient and this time it's no different. His bruises and burns are healing nicely. His headaches seem to have lessened as well, but his nose still hurt like hell. He's thinking a lot clearer since he stopped taking the mystery pills that Svetlana had been giving him.

What were they, anyway?

He knew her intentions were good, but he was surprised she didn't kill him. He still continued taking the antibiotics though, as that's common sense. She's definitely not a pharmacist, or a very trust-worthy vault. When Guy found out they had lost the crypto-locker, and that all of this chaos and death had been for nothing, he was gutted. He could tell she was upset as well, and both were left with an upsetting question.

Where the fuck is it?

I hear someone knock at the door. I look over and see Svetlana enter my apartment, carrying a bag of groceries. She walks over to the table next to the kitchen and puts the bag down, thankfully. She's been extra attentive ever since the discovery of the missing crypto-locker, and I could tell she felt bad. I still can't believe that she and Aria have become friends so quickly, and I'm glad Aria is not alone in her time of grief. Svetlana is grieving in her own way, but it's much different and not as profound, more like being fired from a job you really liked. Oleg left a lot of money behind for her, and now she was free.

Free...but really free?

I can't help myself and am captivated by her beauty again as I see her. She intrigues me on several levels, but the baser ones are winning me over right now, as I imagine what she would look like naked. I believe a woman's body is always such a delightful mystery. I'm intrigued, to say the least, and the unveiling of the truth is always one of my favorite parts.

Plus, I take my time...anticipation.

Svetlana catches me staring and gives me a knowing grin. She enjoys teasing me and it's becoming something she's been doing more and more lately. I'm sure it started out as though she was trying to cheer me up. You know, like wearing sexy clothes as she nursed me back to health. In my defense, I'm a guy, after all, and she knows exactly how to make guys like me smile. It wasn't long before I realized she was craving attention from me, and it was affecting her in ways that were unexpected. There's an undeniable sexual charge between us, but we both know that it is bound to create problems.

Regardless of all that, when it comes to my sexual desires, I will never hesitate to do what comes naturally. And in this case, it was doing Svetlana. I know she feels the same way, but like I said, I like to take my time. I don't know exactly how long I can wait.

As Svetlana is unpacking my groceries, I sneak up from behind, with a rock-hard boner and hungry intentions.

What's the worst that could happen...a slap on the cheek?

She's wearing a sexy little skirt and as she bends over; it hikes up, exposing the edge of her silky panties and that's more than I can handle right now. By the time the vegetables make it to the bottom drawer of the fridge, her ass is barely covered.

What's a Guy to do?

I lose control and grab Svetlana by the waist. Then, spinning her around and locking her lips to mine, she melts readily into my arms. For a guy that likes to take things slow, I find it kind of ironic when my hands grow impatient and begin traveling up, down, and around her dangerous curves. With only a single thought in mind, I find it hard to resist this beautiful woman for much longer. I play this tempting game of seduction, inviting Svetlana to release all inhibition and follow her desires down the path of pleasure and satisfaction, leading to, you guessed it, an earth-shaking conclusion.

I believe we have a common goal.

Svetlana pleasantly surprises me when she drops to her knees, unzipping my pants on the way down. She grabs my ass with one hand and takes a hold of my unyielding dick with the other. Opening her mouth, her tongue immediately travels the distance of my shaft, then twirls its way to the tip, her red lips staining the head of Mr. Ever-Ready.

My hips buck up instinctively, sliding myself further into her mouth, enjoying her eager acceptance. She moans as she takes in my full member, before gagging a moment and then continuing on. Faster and faster, she suctions up and down my sensitive rod, her hand holding my stiffness. She jerks me off as she sucks on my tip and I push her head away with a groan, unwilling to cum.

"Fuck, you're too good at that!"

She looks wickedly up at me, and I see a thousand dirty promises in her Cheshire grin.

I need to take back control!

I get up, removing my shirt, enjoying the way her eyes are trapped on my chest. As she stands, her hands softly rub against my hard muscles, traveling across my pecs and down my abs, to grab my cock again. As she reaches for it, I step back, teasing her, and she gives me a playful pout.

I continue to walk backwards towards my room as she follows. I think we both need this right now, a physical or cathartic release. Too much has been out of our control lately, but this...

This we can control.

She pulls her shirt over her head as she crosses the threshold of my door, and my breath is taken away. She has beautiful breasts that are on full display through the thin fabric of her sexy sheer bra.

I stop walking as the backs of my legs hit my bed, and Svetlana walks up to me, embracing me, her lips slightly parted, expecting a kiss. I plant one on her, then another, and her body melts again into mine. I always forget how much fun it is to make out until I'm making out. There's an urgency in our actions, a hunger that is emerging like a smoldering fire taking light.

I unhook her bra with a deft snap of my fingers, and her girls come out to play. She has beautiful nipples that are getting hard. I help them along, using my tongue as I trace wet circles around them, sucking and nibbling softly, as I grab each breast, enjoying the moans it elicits from her.

I notice her sliding her skirt down and help her along. I use my foot to bring it quickly to the floor. I get another surprised moan. I enjoy the smooth skin of Svetlana's ass and the way the fabric from her thong rubs against my hand as I massage her cheeks, my fingers lingering closer to her wet, wanting sex. Her hips are moving, as she's not used to not getting her way, while not being able to deny the sexual charge it gives her.

I move my hand along her waist and then down the front of the thin material of her panties, happily noticing the heat as my hand moves lower. There is an aching desire we are sharing in this moment, passing this sexually charged energy back and forth, like shaking up a can of soda, and I know things are about to explode. I don't want them to explode too early if you get my drift, so I take charge and turn, still embracing Svetlana, before pushing her roughly to the bed.

She lands on my crumpled blankets, and her eyes light up. She slowly backs away from me before I grab her hips and roughly pull her to the edge of the bed. I go down on my knees, and as I pull her to me, I can't help but notice she smells incredibly good. This drives me crazy, and I lick the insides of her thighs close to the edge of her panties. They barely cover her, and as I lick and kiss the sides of her thighs, I rub my hand over her pussy, massaging her clitoral hood through the sheer fabric.

I think we both can't take the teasing anymore, and I stand up, pulling her soaked panties off, and receiving a grateful moan for my efforts.

Worth it!

I'm back down on my knees in a flash and my mouth hovers above her wet pussy as my tongue finds her clit. Her legs go up instinctively, bent at the knee and I've always found it sexy the way a woman's foot points when they are in pleasure. Her hips buck into me as I suck and work her magical friend gently in my mouth. It's like a remote control that short circuits her brain if done properly and I always look forward to the challenge. As I'm doing this, I slowly slide first one, then two fingers into Svetlana, as she cries out in pleasure, pushing herself onto them further.

There's a real fire building in Svetlana, and I guide her through it, sometimes fast, sometimes achingly slow. But we get there and when we do, let me tell you, it's intense. Her back arches and it's like she's being electrocuted. She cries out over and over in ecstasy, her words sometimes not even making sense.

Right now, Svetlana is in a different place.

I keep her in this state till her eyes roll and then slowly bring her back down to reality. I rub her leg and smile at her as she collects herself, a surprised smile on her relaxed face. She looks me up and down.

"Holy shit, cowboy, you really know how to show a girl a good time."

I smile at this, not sure how to respond to her compliment. I give her another second to catch her breath, then cock my head to the side, with an "Are you ready?" smile on my face.

"Oh, hell ya!"

She responds, and I move to get on top of her before she takes control, straddling me. She wants to ride me and I'm more than happy to oblige, us both moaning as I penetrate her wet pussy. She takes me all, sliding down until we are one, then stays there for a moment, eyes closed, enjoying the sensation. She grinds her hips around and I help her out by rubbing my finger against her clit as she does this. Her movements get faster and more urgent the further we go down this path and soon she's climaxing again, her hand in her hair, the other on my chest.

We both are now sweating, and I flip her back down so I'm on top of her. I urgently need to take charge, and I need to take her now. I pump into her, our grunts and moans in unison as we ride together closer and closer to an explosive climax. She erupts and I do too a second later, pulling out of her at the last minute to spray cum all over her stomach with a grateful moan.

We collapse into each other and lay there for a moment, enjoying the post - coital bliss of just being present in the moment.

...and the moment not sucking...

We come back to earth, and both start laughing as we lay there tangled in a big sweaty mess. I feel the stress rolling off me like the tide, and I feel like I'm smiling for the first time in a long time.

Now for a shower.

Chapter Thirty-Six

When Nora saw Bunny was staying overnight for an early morning treatment, she knew she had to return the collar to her caretaker for safe keeping. She didn't want the spa to be responsible for such a high-priced thing.

It's as garish as it is ostentatious!

She's dreading the thought of having to deliver it, but she could trust this to no one else. Still, it was such a horrible confrontation the last time she was there. And even though she will never admit it to another soul, she's having a hard time with killing Janse. It was so sudden she hadn't really thought, just acted. She was pretty sure her old self reacted instantly, and marveled at how the brain works.

I guess you will never go away, Sandy Sherman, from Ohio. We might as well learn to live with each other.

"What a life!"

She says to no one in particular, tutting as she shakes her head. She puts the collar in her purse, idly thinking this will probably be the most expensive thing she would ever have in there. She has a fleeting thought of running away like in the movies, but then sees herself being run down, a fugitive, her hair all a mess in the helicopter searchlights.

That just would not do!

Well, off to see that horrible woman, I guess. Poor Bunny.

When she had found out the rumors were true about the will placing that large amount of money in the dog's paws, so to speak, she discreetly checked if she could somehow get the conservatorship of the dog, and the money. Unfortunately, all members of the Fowler line would need to be deceased before the courts would look at outside parties. She kept the paperwork just in case, more out of habit than hope.

Nora climbs into her little electric car, her *"work trolley"* she calls it, and plugs the address into her navigation system. She enjoys driving through this swanky part of town, admiring the magnificent houses.

One day...

She tells herself as she settles into her drive. The weather has been turning colder lately, and the news said that the mountains could expect a snow storm at any time. She loves the snow and the holidays that come with it. She turns on a song from her dashboard screen and pulls out of the parking lot, heading up to the Fowler mansion. She laughs at the thought that this has to be the only house owned by a dog.

After six decent songs and three bad ones, Nora pulls into the Fowler mansion driveway and parks her car. Getting out, she stretches and shivers slightly at the cold. This would be a great night for something warm to drink, hopefully spiked with something else to warm her up. She giggles to herself for her silly humor and walks up to the door. After last time, this visit better not be traumatic. Adjusting the front of her shirt, Nora rings the bell and steps back, her purse held tightly to her side.

The snow has begun and the wind swirls some behind her as the door opens. The funny bird looking woman looks fearfully at her as they lock eyes.

"Hello again."

"Um, hello?"

Nora waits a moment, looking expectantly at this odd woman. She's cold and would like to come inside, as this is not a drop at the door type of situation. After a moment of the bespeckled woman's dumb silent gaze, Nora shakes her head.

"May I come in? I have something that I need to return to Mrs. Fowler."

Nora clears her throat.

"Please?"

The wind blows again and Nora, shaking her head, moves past the funny woman into the front hall, stamping her feet as if there was snow already on them. Birdy turns and speaks.

"I'm Birdy Fowler. Give whatever you have to me."

"Thank you, dear, but I really must give this directly to Bunny's conservator."

Nora can see that Birdy is struggling with this.

"If you get her for me, I will be ever so grateful."

With this, she smiles at Birdy. She clasps her hands in front of herself and smiles, showing that she can wait. Birdy has no choice and leaves the room, almost as if in a trance, and not sure what had just happened. A few minutes later, she returns with her cousin, who enters the hall with an expression that is hard for Nora to read. They walk up to her, and old Sandy Sherman screams in her ear that something is not right.

***

Aria can't let the missing crypto-locker go. Her sister died because of this thing, and now it's in the wind. Who could have taken it?

The list of suspects is small, but she can't believe that it somehow ended up back with the Fowlers. There really is no one else she can think of, unless there is someone involved that she doesn't know about. Aria doesn't like that thought, but quickly dismisses it for lack of credible evidence. It has to be with them, and that thought makes her feel like she's holding caustic acid in her mouth.

She forcefully exhales her breath, then gets up and crosses the room to pick up her phone. Svetlana didn't come home last night, and Aria is extra protective with her current grief state. She texts her friend and then smiles when she texts back a few minutes later.

Messaging back and forth, the girls both can't let this go. Between the lurid details of her last 24 hours, Svetlana promises Aria she will talk to Guy. As they continue to text, Aria shares she's worried that Guy will not be ready or want to help. They had known each other for a long time, but this was a whole new level of craziness that surpassed anything they had ever faced before.

Svetlana again promises to talk to Guy and then says good-bye to her friend as she hears the shower stop. When Guy comes out in a towel wrapped around his waist, Svetlana smiles appreciatively at him, holding his gaze. He smiles back but can tell something is on her mind.

"What's up Svet? I can see those gears turning."

"Aria and I want to get the crypto-locker back. This is not fair, and they don't deserve it! They don't deserve to win! I know you're still healing and probably don't want to.."

Guy doesn't let her finish that sentence as he interrupts her.

"I'm in! When are we doing this?"

Svetlana feels pleasantly surprised and marvels once again at this strange man. She has met no one like Guy before and wonders if she ever will again. She calls Aria and they make a plan to meet up at Guy's before heading to the Fowler mansion.

As they get dressed, Svetlana questions Guy.

"How do you think they stole the locker from here?"

This has been bothering her especially, and it makes Svetlana feel like it's her fault. Guy looks up at her with danger in his eyes, momentarily taking her aback as she sees a new side of him.

"THEY stole it. THEY are responsible for ending Oleg and Avery's lives. THEY destroyed your house and broke into mine... THEY kidnapped Aria and I, and most of all THEY pulled me into this shitstorm in the beginning and that triggered everything... no, THIS.."

He brings his pointer finger down into his palm for emphasis.

"THIS all ends tonight."

Alley looks up from her bed, giving Mr. Pig a break. Even she sensed the danger seeping into the room like a lethal mist. She sits up, toy forgotten for the moment as she knows what's going to happen next. The pack is going hunting. Aria arrives a few minutes later and they all stand in Guy's small living room, conspiratorially plotting their next move. Aria smiles at Guy and begins.

"I'm done with your whole weird ride share thing and rented us an SUV."

Guys smiles and shakes his head appreciatively as he looks down. He puts his hands up in an *"I surrender"* type of gesture.

"Guilty as charged!"

He laughs, then continues.

"Smart move Aria! I wonder how many times I've said that to you over the years?"

She rolls her eyes and looks over to Svetlana, who is smiling, enjoying the back and forth, and replies.

"Too many! Why do I even hang out with you?"

She laughs but remembers an awkward teenage girl who was too smart for her own good, and a cute neighbor boy who always seemed to see past that. It was never sexual, more familial with a comfort only a genuine friend can give you. They lock eyes and a darker memory flash of a night when she was attacked by a handsy date and Guy appearing out of nowhere, throttling the guy until she actually felt bad for him. He smiles that boyish grin he somehow maintained, and she momentarily doesn't feel as alone. He then turns serious.

"Ok. If we're going to do this, we need to be fast and decisive. What is our objective?"

He looks between the girls and notices that Alley has come over and is sitting at his side. He absently plays with her fury ears and soft fur as they ponder the obvious. Svetlana is the first to break.

"To get the crypto-locker, duh."

Guy nods his head and smiles.

"True, but how? I'm tired of the violence, but I want to re-claim what was stolen. I can let Doc's widow go, chalk the kidnapping up to grief. That motherfucker Janse is worm food, so that box is happily checked. Texas is not worth it and probably doesn't even know where she is. I say we go in, make it clean. I watch the women as you two search the house."

Alley barks, startling them and Guy jokes.

"Okay, while you THREE search the house...happy?"

He looks down at Alley, thankful for the temporary distraction. She pants happily, looking back up with adoration in her eyes. As he looks back up, both girls nod their head in agreement. Everyone is wearing their game face right now, which he's pleased to see. They are about to dance on the edge of a razorblade and try not to get cut. This never works, but he tells himself this time will be different. He checks to make sure his gun is securely in his holster, behind his back, as his mind tells him that was just a lie.

He puts a few more full mags in his coat pocket, and they are out the door a minute later. The snow is really falling now. As they drive to the mansion, they fine tune the plan and try to foresee any complications. As they park and get out, they have no way of knowing that Jenny had hired another company from Harriet Fowler's dark network.

Guy's old buddies from Green Tactical Solutions.

Chapter Thirty-Seven

The adrenaline before a fight is a funny thing. To me, it feels like I hit my funny bone mixed with a little nausea. The crazy thing is that when it buzzes through me, I revel in the feeling. I don't want to admit it, but a dark part of me is always looking forward to the fight. I'm feeling that way now as we walk up to the door. I'm mad and the worst part is that I'm justified, so it's harder to control.

"Remember, no violence if we can help it. Let's get this thing and then get gone. Bing bang boom."

I'm saying this mostly to myself, as the girls nod earnestly at that. I feel the group pulling strength from each other for the upcoming encounter. Alley is right by my side, ever faithful, ever on guard, sniffing the air. We step up to the door and I check to see if it's unlocked. It's not, but thirty seconds later, that is not the case as we enter the Fowler mansion, with money on our minds. I put my lock pick set back into my back pocket and readjust my gun. I never pull it out unless I'm going to use it, so for now, it sleeps in well-worn leather, dreaming fifteen lethal, little, hollow-point nightmares.

We can hear an argument from deeper in the house and slowly creep toward the sound. I'm getting closer when I hear Nora James's voice. She sounds like she's keeping her cool, but there definitely is a panicked quality about it. That puts my threat analysis up a notch, as I have never heard her sound like this before.

She's always in control.

"Oh, you just wait. You didn't think you could just come in here like you did nothing wrong."

I recognize that bird squawk anywhere and pick up my pace, rounding the corner and startling all three women, as I reply.

"Yeah, I think she did. Why? What do you have in mind?"

Jenny recovers first and looks over at her cousin, her look slowly turning to disgust. Texas is standing frozen in place, shoulders hunched, and urine running down the inside of her leg, soaking her bedazzled jeans. I look over at her, and our eyes lock.

"Oh yeah, your value just skyrocketed, Texas!"

Alley lets out a growl from beside me and the low rumble moves through the room like a primal judge. She sees the sparkling mess and barks once.

At this, Birdy's already white face drains what little color it had left, and she falls like a sack of rocks, her nervous system throwing in the piss-soaked towel. We look from the wet pile of Texas to the shocked looking Jenny. She can only shake her head, looking aghast as she hunches her shoulders in an *"I don't know"* gesture.

"Nora, are you ok?"

I ask this as my eyes lock with the terrified Mrs. James and I can see that she really isn't. This could have all ended rather badly for her and the reality of it is slapping her in the face like a jealous lover. She can only shake her head as she tries not to cry.

Svetlana crosses over to her, and a moment later Aria does as well. I absently wonder if this is a female pack thing, subconsciously acted out, ingrained from generations of needing to do this for safety. I'm not that smart, but I can see that it brings Nora some comfort, and that's good enough for me.

We all look back at the moaning pile of Birdy that is just coming to. Before that happens, the adults decide to have a conversation. Jenny looks between the four of us and I can see the warring emotions swirling through her brain. The women, for their part, stare menacingly at her before I nod and they set off, Nora following behind, looking for our wayward crypto-locker. Nora calls for Alley, and she looks at me before following, ears swiveling, hyper aware.

Jenny watches them leave smart enough to keep her mouth shut. When they are gone, she turns her head to look at me, and I see the same old burning hate.

"I get you hate me because of Doc."

"His name was Frank!"

"Frank then, I get why you hate me, and I get why you wanted to get the money, but why work with that total psychopath Boogie Nights?"

She smiles despite herself momentarily at the nickname, but the moment is fleeting and passes almost as soon as it begun.

Janse.

She's wondered the same thing, but trusted the man who set it up, an old friend of the family, or so he said. What was his name again?

Oh ya, Jahvey Simbado.

***

When Janse was killed, it had ruined a carefully laid out plan, one by Mr. Jahvey Simbado. He had found out about the money when the protection order was to be received and worked quickly to turn a member of Harriet's inner circle. Janse Ulrickson was known to the agency because he was a psychopath for hire, and they had used him a few times in the past. It was easy to get him to turn on Harriet and even easier to use the gullible Svetlana to find out that the crypto-locker was stored in the home safe.

But the raid, he fucked up the raid!

Jahvey is still pissed that Janse escalated things so much during their attempted seizure of the crypto-locker. He asked him to get the device, not kill everyone and burn down the whole goddamn house.

Everyone around me is completely incompetent!

He thought that when he forced Guy to accept the mission, it would be a done deal. Everyone knew Guy left the agency because he was completely burned out. The fact that he has been such a thorn in their side is unbelievable and just keeps ratcheting up Jahvey's hate for this man. He would like to think of them as rivals, but deep down he knows Guy doesn't even consider them equal.

Well, fuck that guy. The money is mine!

He thinks this last thought as the SUV he's riding in stops in front of two vehicles in the oversized parking area in front of the Fowler Mansion. Three more like it pull in behind and mercenaries pour out. Within a minute, it looks like a bad-guy convention, and they all look to Jahvey to give the signal. He pulls a funny-looking grenade with a bunch of holes around a metal sleeve from his vest and pulls the pin. He looks back at his men, who are stacking into lines to rush in, and nodding to himself, opens the door. He tosses the flashbang grenade inside, then retreats quickly back around the door frame. Everyone around instinctively holds their mouths slightly open and counts backwards from five.

The party is about to begin.

Chapter Thirty-Eight

I hear a metal object skipping along the wood floor, making a skidding and scrapping sound. I'm wondering what it is, when a loud bang and an incredibly bright flash explodes from the hallway. The over pressure from the blast knocks pictures off the wall and blows papers from the table next to where we are standing. Our ears pop and I instinctively fall to the floor, pulling out my weapon.

The flashbang is designed to incapacitate a group of people in a lightning raid style situation, but my training kicked in instantly. From the floor, I orientate my weapon's muzzle down the hallway, ignoring my screaming middle ear. I can hear Alley bark from the floor above me, giving me some clue as to where my friends are. A thin gauze of smoke hangs in the hallway as the smoke detector starts beeping and I know this song all too well.

"Girls, hide!"

I'm pulling the trigger a moment later, sending rounds down the hall and into the door and frame as shapes burst through the fatal funnel. Some fall, but my magazine runs dry before the tap of human bullshit pouring into the mansion can be turned off. I wrist flick my pistol, flinging out the empty mag, before slamming in a fresh one.

Let's play motherfuckers!

I'm requiring the far hall through my sights when I'm struck by two almost simultaneous observations that rock me harder than if I would have been shot. The first is I see one of the baddies I shot, moaning and squirming around in the hall. He's distinctly wearing a Green Tac solutions vest and patch.

These guys again!

If that wasn't bad enough, I recognized the voice shouting orders from outside the door. Of course, that shitbird would send in others first to do his dirty work. Well good, Jahvey, you saved me the trouble of having to find your dumb ass later.

Now it really is game on, because if he's here, it means he set me up. He ultimately is the architect of my current situation, the creator of my pain, the one responsible for Avery's death, and all this.

"Jahvey!"

I yell this as I get to my feet, my anger getting the best of me. I see him ducking in past the door and barely miss him as my rounds slam into the wall inches from his ear. He looks momentarily at me, startled, and I hope he's picking up what I'm putting down.

"Jahvey, you motherfucker, I'm going to end you! No games, no bullshit, no more shit talking, you fuck! You set me up! You hurt my friends and took one from me... You crossed too many lines. And tonight it's payback!"

I hear him curse to himself but have to duck back in the room as someone fires blindly around the corner. I feel one bullet pass harmlessly through the fabric of my pants leg, knowing I will feel the shock from that later. Jahvey tries to sound tough and say something, but he keeps stumbling over his words. I think the lazy bastard forgot to continue to train when he started driving that desk...

Oops! You moron, I'm not surprised.

His loss is my gain. I peek back around the corner, ready to shoot at him again when I run into a startled mercenary who was creeping up the hall towards me. He brings his weapon up and I quickly step to the side, helping him and slamming his now hurling weapon straight into his dumb startled face. As I hear a crunch and feel him go limp, I grab and spin him, using his body as a shield as I move down the hallway, firing the remaining rounds in his rifle. He shudders as rounds impact all around us, exploding into the walls and floor as I rush down the hall. I get to the end when the gun runs dry and throw the now dead mercenary into his startled friends.

The smoke is getting thicker, and a small part of my brain acknowledges that the house is now on fire.

Insurance companies probably have a wanted poster of me somewhere.

The hallway is now truly chewed up, and the fire is climbing the wall from the rug, which now lies engulfed in flame at the bottom. I hear Texas calling out to Jenny from behind me and hope they don't have any weapons, or I'm in a terrible spot. I retreat out the front door and cough; the smoke beginning to thicken as it pours out the entrance.

The snow is swirling now, falling in a million different angles, and my old scars are burning to come out and play. I struggle for a moment, overcome by the current feelings I'm experiencing and the creeping sensation of a burning cabin. From out of nowhere, I hear Reaper yell, as if right beside me.

"Remember who you are...contact front!"

Like a heavy metal door slamming down, everything that is not lethal folds back within my soft, little cozy self, and I robotically crouch after kicking the door in. I'm through it before it even slams against the wall and catch two mercs completely by surprise as they poke at their unfortunate buddies. A moment later, they are all holding hands in Valhalla, and I move over their surprised corpses.

I push back into the house, this time a tactical machine instead of a creeping scared civilian, and dominated the situation. Having the element of surprise, I clear my way further into the mansion before I'm stopped by a hail of bullets from an upstairs loft balcony. Jahvey has turtled up there and is shooting at anything that is moving. Seeing the bodies lying there, his own people, I find a lower level to hate him on.

What a complete piece of shit!

Chapter Thirty-Nine

While the gun battle rages around them, a terrified Jenny and Texas lock eyes. This is too much, and neither one of them was prepared for any of this. They wanted the money, and it seemed like a simple thing, really. How was Jenny supposed to know all of this would happen?

I just wanted to be happy.

She now knows that was naïve but still hopes for the best. When she learned from Nora James about the collar code, she had removed the other collar she wore around her wrist and discovered a code there as well. How stupid she thinks, she didn't notice this before, and mentally chastises herself yet again for her epic screw up with all of this. Birdy is supposed to be the one who is notorious for her screw ups, but this sits squarely on Jenny's shoulders. She looks across the room at Birdy, both of them huddled on the floor, and each clutching a custom-made dog collar so hard their knuckles are turning white. Jenny jerks her head in a *"follow me"* gesture and then crawls out the room through the other door. As she moves across the floor, bullets are ripping through the wall above her and debris rains down like a bunch of invisible workmen are drilling holes.

She reaches the door and discovers that Texas wasn't following her. She sticks her head back into the room and yells at her cousin.

"Get over here stupid, move your ass!"

This gets Texas moving and they both scoot through the door and into the next room. Jenny is heading for the study and hopes that Texas doesn't get lost along the way. They get up and run down the side hall and into the study below the master loft. Smoke mists through the air, and now multiple smoke detectors are competing for attention. The terrified women can hear shooting from close by and jump each time they hear a shot.

Harriet Fowler's study looked like something out of an old school gangster movie. She had the globe bar, the leather couches, the oversized desk with the multiple bookshelves containing books she had never read. It also contains the safe and Jenny rushes over to it as she calls out over her shoulder.

"Watch the door, Birdy."

Birdy is too caught up in the money and disregards her shocked cousin, continuing to follow her to the safe, a maniacal gleam in her eyes. Jenny opens the safe and then is startled as she feels her sweaty cousin right behind her, looking over her shoulder.

She's literally breathing in my ear.

"Birdy! I told you to watch the door."

"No way! So, you can cut me out of the money? I know what you're up to!"

It's true Jenny was planning to turn on Texas and is surprised that she figured it out. With an annoyed huff, Jenny pulls the crypto-locker from the safe and they both examine it.

A metal case about the size of a pack of cigarettes. The crypto-locker was designed to begin its funneling and transfer function when it was plugged into a computer and the codes were input into a pop-up text box. At least, that's what Jenny had learned when she studied everything she could find on the subject. The problem with inference is that you don't know...what you don't know. And in this case, Jenny did not know about the failsafe. A small piece of metal with a cable that plugged into the other port on the device. Svetlana didn't know to grab this, when she took the crypto-locker from Oleg's safe. Both collars must be connected to the clip, magnetizing it and sending an unlock signal to the device, which neutralizes the high yield micro explosive contained inside.

With her bird-like cousin gawking over her shoulder, Jenny carefully inputs the codes from the collars into the appropriate fields. As she's about to input the last character, she looks back at her weird cousin and all is forgiven. They are about to be very rich and none of this will matter anymore; they won. With a triumphant flair, Jenny pushes the last key.

And the light turns red.

Chapter Forty

"Why don't you come up here and get me, tough guy!"

"Fuck you, Jahvey!"

I'm really getting sick of this little weasel now; he's like a fucked-up hemorrhoid, always ruining my day. I'm starting to think I'm going to have to do something stupid when the room below him violently explodes. Lethal wood pieces, both big and small spray the area, hurtled from the rapid kinetic disassembly event that had just happened. My ears are ringing after the most painful pop, and I hear as if through a muted fuzz. As I get up, I realize I wasn't even aware I had been knocked over and worry about a concussion.

What happened?

I can hear Jahvey moaning and walk towards him. He lies on the broken wood, back clearly broken with burning chunks of wood smoldering all around him; there is smoke everywhere now. He's reaching around, blindly grasping for help, covered in wood shrapnel, bleeding from a hundred different places, fear in his eyes, and I think, good!

As I stand over him, wobbling slightly, he tries to say something, but I have heard enough. No drama, no speeches, no windy movie monologues, not this time. With two quick shots into his heaving chest, I end his miserable life.

Now to go find my friends.

Waving my hand in front of me, I cough as I realize the smoke is really thickening. As I move back the way I came, the smoke continues to intensify until I must crawl through it, looking for the stairs. I'm calling out to the women and so far,; I have heard nothing. I'm getting worried and my maniacal brain paints the worst scenarios in my mind. I shake my head, trying to knock out the intrusive thoughts, and push on.

I spot the steps and hurry over to them, coughing and calling out to my friends. As I make the second-floor landing, I stand and strain my ears, listening for any sound out of the ordinary. You don't have to hear everything, just the thing that doesn't belong. In this case, I hear a muffled cough, and rush to my right towards the location I think it came from. From out of the smoke, a mercenary suddenly appears, knife in hand. He gets the drop on me, but that's all. As he lunges in, I aikido his ass, and he ends up crying on the floor with a broken arm. I continue over him, bursting into the room, coming face to face with a terrified Nora James. She has soot on her face and tear streaks have washed narrow valleys through it, down the landscape of her face. She's shaking and clinging onto a panicking Alley. They both rush me as soon as they see me, Nora hugging me and Alley running into my leg, leaning against it, yet still alert and looking around. Always alert, what an amazing dog. She was protecting Nora.

I point Nora in the right direction and ask her to take Alley to safety. I then head deeper into the second floor, looking for the girls. It's dark and with the smoke following me; it seems downright supernatural.

This shit's giving me the creeps.

"Aria! Svetlaaaaana!"

I call their names as I continue to search, fighting my instinct and common sense, telling me to get out before the whole place goes up. I'm really starting to panic now and pick up my pace.

"Guy!"

I stop and instantly change direction, heading down the hall I was just passing. This place is a maze. I hope I can find my way out. I hear something explode downstairs and my concern doubles with a side order of panic. I force myself to not rush as I continue to search, but just barely.

I see Aria crouching, leaning against the wall, and hurry towards her. She's coughing and tears stream from her eyes. The smoke is thickening even up here, and I worry I'm beginning to hear crackling. I put my arm around her and help her get up, staying against the wall.

"Ari, *cough. Where is Svet?"

She points down the dark hallway, coughing.

"We separated to cover more ground. She went that way."

I desperately look around but realize the way I came is no longer an option as the smoke is too thick and I can see flashes of light flickering within it. I move back into the room and look out the window. There is no roof, just a really tall two-story drop. We scramble back out into the hall and move down to the end, where I see another window. This one has a roof on the other side, and I waste no time breaking the glass with a nearby chair. I clear the remaining shards from the frame and help Aria out. We look at each other from our separate sides of the window, and I see a different panic in Aria's eyes.

"Don't worry Ari, I'm coming back, and I'll have Svet with me. Get off this roof while you can and find Nora and Alley."

"You better."

Our eyes lock again, and a lifetime of bonds passes between us. With that...she starts her way, and I head for mine. Once more unto the breach, dear friends.

Once more.

Again, I roll the dice and push my luck, dashing into the dark, calling out to Svetlana. I'm almost at the end of the hall before I hear her cough. Within thirty seconds I find her, crouched over by a door frame. As I reach her, I joke.

"Just like old times, huh?"

I realize from the look she gives me that my joke was not funny.

"Sorry, let's get out of here."

She coughs again and gives me the let's go signal, panic in her eyes. Ok, let's go...

But where?

I guess a window is as good as anything, so we head inside the room, and thankfully have a roof on the other side of this window as well. A minute later and we're on the roof, looking for a way down. As we are walking across, we see Nora, and she waves to us.

Just then, a series of explosions erupt throughout the house, and we are thrown off balance. From Nora's point of view, she witnesses something that she will never forget. Guy catches Svetlana by her outstretched arm and they are both backlit by a series of explosions, creating a silhouetted image that takes her breath away.

We quickly recover and are able to find a safe way down a moment later. We link up with Nora, Aria, and Alley, the last who runs up barking when she sees me. We all huddle for a minute, hugging and exchanging thanks for the others' safety. We leave a moment later as the fire trucks pass us, speeding in.

Chapter Forty-One

"Remember me and smile, for it's better to forget than to remember me and cry."

~Dr. Suess

Avery always loved Dr. Suess.

We are all wearing black when we meet up. It's been a week since the incident at the Fowler Mansion, and it was still hard to believe it was all over. We could now look back on the events that had pulled and shaped us. We were iron forged by the fire of these experiences and emerged as steel. Lifelong bonds were built, and shared pain was felt, as we navigated this, but we navigated it together. I look around the group and I'm so thankful to these people that fell into my life. I look at Nora James, good old Hatchet. When we first met, we were oil and water, but now I look at her as an almost maternal figure, with a deep mutual respect. She was terrified throughout this experience, but she stuck it out, always for the good of the group. Standing next to her is Svetlana, my friend and confidante. My mission was to protect her, now a free and very rich woman. We shared an experience that few will ever understand, a bond built not of blood, but of blood spilled. The violence we withstood and the attempts on our lives had created a unique bond that was larger than love. There is nothing like the looming fate of death to make a person really want to live to.

Standing next to Svetlana is Aria. My oldest friend, Corn-flakes, my little sister, and lifetime bestie. Again, she proved her unyielding friendship, following me through the fires of hell, getting burned badly along the way. Her heart is breaking, and it breaks mine even more. I thought that was not possible and again feel what infinite means. The cold vacuum that threatens to consume you if you let it. This is where the ghosts are born, and where the spirits come to dance and play.

Aria has me, but Svetlanas friendship has really been the helping factor I can tell. She needs another sister, as harsh as that sounds. Not to replace Avery, as nothing could ever do that. But Aria is suffering from half of her soul being ripped away and anything that can lend some weight to that wound is helpful. Aria will recover. She's tough, and she's smart, plus she now has a pet.

After the whole incident, Nora had shown up at the girl's apartment with a gift.

A cute little dog named Bunny.

The dog needed a new home and Nora could think of nobody better. She knew it was the right thing to do the moment she handed the small dog to Aria and saw her smile. Nora had indeed been awarded emergency conservatorship for the billionaire dog and planned on donating a sizeable chunk to her favorite animal charities.

Care of Bunny, of course.

And speaking of dogs, I look down and pet the soft fur on Alleys' head. She looks up at me and licks my hand. We are a funny pair, but we have become a family. I didn't realize how much I needed companionship until it appeared in my lap, literally. As I have gotten to know her better, I can tell there is something extremely special about this dog. It's as if she understands more than she should have, a lot of the time. I know dogs can be smart, but this seems, I don't know...

Next level?

I'm pulled from that thought as Aria speaks. She has tears in her eyes, looking at us as we all stand around each other. We are on a beautiful cliff, overlooking the ocean and the sun is hitting the water, setting fire to the sky.

"This spot, this...my sister loved this spot. When I knew she was thinking through something and needed a place to go, this was it. She was..."

Aria sobs, unable to continue. I hug her in my arms, a tight hug to show her she's not alone. I then look up, and continue for her, trying to be the best torch bearer of Avery's spirit in all this darkness, as we try to say goodbye.

"She was an amazing woman of many talents, but her finest was how she always looked out for her sister. They were twins, but Avery always put Aria first and it was something I admired about her."

I feel Aria cry harder into my shirt, and take a moment, giving her space to feel her loss. This is how we grieve, in pieces that break from us. It's our souls saying goodbye and it fucking sucks. Svetlana rubs Arias back.

"You're not alone. We are here. We will always be here for you."

I look up and see my ghosts standing behind my friends and know that statement could not be more true. Good or bad, this is my family, and this is my fate. My soul might continue to burn, but the inferno has died down. I will always have my ghosts but through time I hope to learn to live with them, because I'm done fighting, and I can't run anymore.

We all then take out a small bag containing some of the cremated remains of Avery and free her in the wind.

Please be at peace, Avery...

Chapter Forty-Two

List of U.S. Government and Military Acronyms

NATO - The North Atlantic Treaty Organization

HUMINT - Human Intelligence (Intel gathering category)

Sapper - A specialized Combat Engineer who has passed the Sapper Leadership Course.

LP/OP - Listening Post and Observation Post.

Pogey bait - Snacks and candy not issued or found in traditional rations.

BDU - Battle Dress Uniform

Chapter Forty-Three

A.C. Meyer is a proud 100% permanently disabled combat veteran, and multi-disciplined artist, whose work has appeared in numerous galleries and events for over 30 years. With over 20 years of combined experience with the things he writes about, his personal journey has been just as dynamic and unusual as the stories he creates. Outside of work, he enjoys hanging out with loved ones, volunteering with veteran causes, camping, and he's a hardcore gamer. He lives in Colorado with his family and multiple pets.

Susan Segovia-Munoz is from Los Angeles, California. Learning from the bottom up and always the hard way, self-taught and streetwise, it is finally her time to shine. She is the author of the Sweet Melissa Memoir Series, an inspirational story of self-destruction – continuously failing and falling, yet overcoming adversity while struggling with the stigma of mental illness, incarceration and addiction. Susan has recently finished her first screenplay, The Mark, which was inspired by some of her own life experiences. She met A.C. Meyers on LinkedIn, clicked, and they immediately became writing partners for the project: Soul on Fire: A Guy Castle Psychological Thriller.

Chapter Forty-Four

The Sweet Melissa Memoir Series

Ignorance is Not Bliss

What's So Sweet About Melissa?

Behind Bars

Destination Unknown

Caged But Free

Shine On You Crazy Junkie